IN A HOTEL GARDEN

Other Books by Gabriel Josipovici

The Book of God: A Response to the Bible

The Mirror of Criticism: Selected Reviews

Text & Voice: Essays

The World & the Book: A Study of Modern Fiction

IN A HOTEL GARDEN

GABRIEL JOSIPOVICI

A NEW DIRECTIONS BOOK

Manufactured in the United States of America
New Directions Books are printed on acid-free paper
First published in Great Britain in 1993 by Carcanet Press Limited.
First published as New Directions Paperbook 801 in 1995.
Published simultaneously in Canada by Penguin Books Canada Limited.

Library of Congress Cataloging-in-Publication Data

Josipovici, Gabriel, 1940-
In a hotel garden / Gabriel Josipovici.
  p. cm.
  ISBN 0-8112-1291-2 (pbk.)
  I. Title.
PR6060.064148   1995   95-1316
823'.914—dc20   CIP

New Directions Books are published for James Laughlin
by New Directions Publishing Corporation,
80 Eighth Avenue, New York 10011

To Jeffrey Newman

'Potiphar's wife too wished to belong to
the history of Israel.'

Midrash on Genesis 39

Contents

IN A HOTEL GARDEN

I   The Postcard

They climb up Putney Hill towards the Heath. The dog, as always, strains at the lead, anxious to be free, then veers unexpectedly sideways and buries his nose in the gutter.

– Come on Em! Rick says, tugging at the lead. Come on boy!

– Twelve miles, Ben says. Twelve bloody miles. Can you believe it?

– Come *on*! Rick says, pulling harder.

The dog, his hind legs on the pavement, his nose in the gutter, refuses to budge.

– Can you believe it? Ben asks.

Abruptly the dog loses interest in the smell and surges forward again, dragging Rick after him.

– Here boy, Rick says. Easy. Easy.

– Twelve bloody miles, Ben says.

– How did you know it was twelve? Rick asks him.

– One of the drivers told us.

– You mean coming the other way? Rick says. He stopped and told you?

– No no, Ben says. It was on the radio. Everybody had their doors open and their radios on. People were walking about and talking. Some had even taken their camping chairs out of their cars and were sitting on the side of the road, drinking cans of beer.

The dog lurches sideways again, wrapping the lead round Ben's legs.

– No! Rick says, dragging him back. No!

– It must have been around a hundred in the shade, Ben says, stepping free of the lead and going round to the other side of his friend. You could feel the heat rising up from the tarmac.

Rick winds the lead round his wrist and pulls the dog against his legs.

– Are you going to behave or aren't you? he asks him, bending over him and willing the dog to look into his eyes.

– Bits of the road were actually melting, Ben says. Right there. If you stepped on them the tar came away on the soles of your shoes.

– Are you? Rick asks, his face still only a few inches from the dog's.

– There wasn't a single tree in sight, Ben says. Just this flat plain with the pylons rising out of it and the road and the heat sort of pressing down on you from above.

They move forward again, the dog panting as the collar cuts into his neck, his front paws scrabbling to get a grip on the pavement.

Rick stops.

– Sit! he says sharply.

The dog looks round at him over his shoulder.

– Sit! he says again.

The dog lowers his behind a little.

– Sit!

Reluctantly the dog lowers his behind to within a few inches of the pavement.

– Nobody, Ben says, even so much as –

– Come on! Rick says, taking his friend's arm as the traffic at the top of the hill eases momentarily. The dog, sensing freedom, makes a dash for the other side, pulling his master who in turn pulls his friend.

– Nobody, Ben says, even so much as raised his voice. Nobody complained. They just settled down to wait as if it was the most natural thing in the world.

– Here, Rick says. He bends down, holding the dog between his knees and feeling under the fur of his neck for the collar. – Here, he says again, as he snaps off the lead.

The dog, released, streaks off into the bushes.

The two men begin to walk again, as Rick hangs the lead round his neck and stuffs the ends into the v-neck of his pullover.

– Go on, he says.

– Oh, Ben says, it's not very interesting.

– No no. Go on.

Ben walks beside him in silence.

– You caught the boat all right though? Rick asks, stopping and looking round for the dog.

– You're joking, Ben says.

– You missed it?

– We missed that one, Ben says, and we missed the next one as well, because there'd been an accident on the roundabout outside Ostend and that held us up for another half hour. There wasn't any room on the one

11

after that, so we eventually took off at half past four in the morning. Only sixteen hours late.

Rick stops again and whistles for the dog, who appears at once, wagging his tail and grimacing as he ambles up to them. As he draws near he suddenly picks up speed and dashes past them, his nose to the ground, and vanishes into the bushes again.

The two men resume their walk.

– She kept saying we should have flown, Ben says. You know how she is when she gets going. She didn't say anything about flying when we were whistling along with the windows open and the sun on our backs. She only got going about planes when we were stuck in that jam. And then she didn't stop. Even the train would have been better, she said. At least there are lavatories on trains. As if I'd arranged for this to happen.

Rick stops suddenly and Ben, who has carried on walking and talking, turns and retraces his steps. Rick whistles, looking round for the dog.

Ben, standing beside him now, joins in the whistling.

– Em Em Em Em Em! Rick calls, in the voice he only uses for calling the dog. Em Em Em Em Em!

The dog appears, running along the path towards them.

– Where the hell were you? Rick asks, bending and looking him in the eye.

The dog looks up at him sheepishly.

– You swine, Rick says quietly.

The dog sits abruptly, wagging his tail in the dust.

Ben crouches beside his friend, then slowly raises his hands in front of him, his fingers curved into claws, and advances on the dog. The dog crouches in turn, watching him carefully.

– Aaaaagh! Ben shouts, leaping forward.

The dog feints, then closes with him.

– Aaaaagh! Ben shouts again, and the two roll together in the grass.

Suddenly the dog yelps, twists out of his grasp and runs away. He stands at a distance looking at them, then turns and hurries down the underpass.

– Coward, Ben says, getting up and brushing the dust and grass off his trousers.

The two friends walk on. They follow the dog down the underpass and re-emerge, walking in the direction of the pond.

– So, Rick says, what time did you finally get home?

– Some time, Ben says. It was day. Another day.

The pond comes into view.

– She went on complaining? Rick says. The whole way?

– More or less, Ben says. You know what she's like when she starts.

They reach the edge of the pond. Rick turns and whistles for the dog, who appears at once, wagging his tail sheepishly and grimacing at him. Rick puts him on the lead again.

They start to walk round the pond. Rick shoos away a large young Dobermann and then a busy little Jack Russell.

– And then? he says.

– I told you, Ben says. When I woke up she was gone.

– When you woke up when?

– It was the middle of the night, Ben says. I imagine it must have been the following night, though it might have been the one after that, by then I'd rather lost track of time, as you can imagine. The flat was quiet. You know that kind of silence, when a place is empty? I couldn't believe it. I really couldn't. It was as though a tap had been opened somewhere and relief was flooding through me. Not happiness. Relief. Like floating on a calm sea and feeling all the tension gradually draining out of your body. I told myself it was only a dream and turned over and went back to sleep. But I think I was smiling like an idiot in my sleep.

They leave the pond and start to walk in the direction of the windmill. After a few yards Rick releases the dog, who immediately dives into the bushes and disappears.

– The next time I woke it was morning, Ben says.

– This morning, Rick says.

– My God, Ben says. Yes. This morning.

– And? Rick says.

They stand back to let two horses and their riders pass them on the narrow path.

Rick begins to walk again, Ben at his side.

– And? Rick says.

– I didn't even go into the bedroom, Ben says. I lay there for a while and tested the silence. I hadn't been mistaken. There was still that sense of emptiness about the flat. I lay there for a while, waiting, but nothing moved, then I got up slowly and carefully and went into the kitchen and made some tea and let it brew and got a mug and put in the milk and sugar and poured in the tea, and meanwhile I'd cut the bread and put it on the grill, all very slow and deliberate, though I didn't light the grill. Then, with my cup of tea in my hand, I went on a tour of inspection.

The dog is there, trotting ahead of them again. Rick quickens his pace and Ben hurries to keep up with him.

14

– The blankets were trailing on the floor, he says. The sheets were bunched up in the middle of the bed as though she'd wrapped them round herself and then kicked them off half a dozen times. The whole room was in chaos. The cupboard was open and half the contents were bursting out of it.

The dog has vanished again. Rick stops and whistles. Nothing happens. He whistles again.

The dog appears from behind them, his muzzle foaming. Rick pats his head.

– Not ordinary chaos, you understand, Ben says. This was theatrical chaos. It was chaos telling you it was chaos. You know what I mean?

Rick has stopped and is busy wiping the saliva off his hand with his handkerchief. Ben turns back to him.

– Every square foot of that room had a message for me, Ben says. And the message was always the same.

– Meaning? Rick says, starting to walk again.

– Meaning you fucked up my life and I've had enough; I'm getting out, Ben says.

– Ah, Rick says.

– I was rather cool actually, Ben says, strolling at his friend's side. I'm quite pleased with the way I handled it. I stood there for a long time, cup in hand, just surveying the scene. I suppose somewhere at the back of my mind was the thought that she might be there somewhere. Under one of the blankets or something. Though I didn't think she was the type. I don't think she ever cared enough either. But these things are in the air. It's the sort of thing people do. They read about Sylvia Plath and it puts ideas into their heads. So after I'd taken a good look from a standing position I started to pad about the room, prodding at the blankets and the bundles of clothes with my foot, looking under the bed, that sort of thing. But she wasn't there. She'd gone. So I strolled back to the kitchen, lit the grill, poured myself another cup of tea, got out the butter and the marmalade, and settled down to a healthy breakfast. Then I ran the water for a bath and had a shave and a good soak. Then I dried myself carefully – I seemed to be doing everything carefully, as though bits of me might snap off if I made a false movement –, put on some clean clothes, folded the bed-things in the living-room where I'd slept, and put them away. Then I just moved through the bedroom with a big dustbin bag, shoving in anything that wasn't mine. I tied the bag shut and put it in the hall to bring round to the PDSA, then I went back into the bedroom, gathering up the rest, which I dumped in the laundry bag. By lunch-time it was all done. You'd never have guessed there'd been anyone but me living in that flat.

They arrive at the windmill. Rick throws himself down on the grass and Ben slowly lowers himself down beside him.

The dog appears out of nowhere, his nose white with dust.

– Come! Ben says. Come Em! Come!

The dog stands panting beside him. Ben gently rubs the dust off his nose, then strokes his head between the ears. The dog collapses beside him, turns over on his back and waves his legs weakly in the air.

– We got your card, Rick says, stretching out and gazing up at the sky.

Ben lies on his stomach, his right arm round the dog.

– It looked fantastic, Rick says. He pulls up a blade of

16

grass and holds it for a while above his face. Finally he puts the tender end in his mouth. – We really must try to get out there with you one of these days, he says.

Ben draws the dog to him, feeling the dog's heart beating wildly in his chest.

– Maybe next year, Rick says, eyes closed, chewing the blade of grass.

Ben and the dog appear to have dropped off to sleep.

– It'll be easier next year, Rick says.

He spits the chewed blade of grass and feels about beside him for another.

– I think Vee's had enough of family holidays, he says.

Ben takes his arm away from the dog, who flops onto his side, breathing heavily.

– Em Em Em Em Em, Ben whispers in his ear. The dog's tail begins to thump against the ground.

– I think I could bribe her to stay and look after Em, Rick says. I reckon if I set about it in the right way she'd be willing. Then there'd just be the two of us and Robert.

Ben in his turn rolls on to his back.

– I'd like to do that walk you told us about in your card, Rick says. The one that goes round those seven peaks.

– Was it that card of the rock glowing in the light of the setting sun? Ben asks him.

– Yes.

– It's incredible, Ben says. Really incredible. The whole of the valley's in darkness and the damn thing's so big the sun must still be catching it, way up there. But it doesn't look as if light's shining *on* it, rather as if it's lit up from the inside. There's just no other way to describe it. Even when you see it you can't believe it.

– I think you sent us the same one last year, Rick says.

– I did?

– I think so, Rick says. Yes.

– Oh God, Ben says.

– No, I'm glad you did. The other one's disappeared. We had it up on the board in the kitchen for ages.

– Oh God, Ben says again.

He gets up and goes into the café in the windmill.

When he comes out the dog is on his feet, wagging his tail and looking at Rick, who is still lying there with the blade of grass sticking up out of his mouth.

– OK, Ben says.

– Rick spits out the blade of grass and gets to his feet.

– Come on boy! he says. Home!

– That's the most spectacular one, Ben says. That's why I sent it to you. But there are nice ones of the woods and some of the church and there's even one of the hotel. But that one's the most spectacular.

– Amazing, Rick says.

The dog trots along at their heels.

II Fish Pie

When they get back to the house Ben says to Francesca:
– I gather I sent you the same card as last year.
   – Did you? she says. I don't remember.
   – The one with the rock glowing in the evening light.
   – Oh yes, Francesca says.
   – Sand's moved out, Rick says.
   – Is that it? she says.
   – Is what it? Ben says.
   – I wondered why you said you'd be on your own, Francesca says.
   – He's relieved, Rick says.
   – Are you? she asks him.
He smiles at her.
   – Are you really?
He nods, grinning.
   – You look pleased enough, she says.
Robert comes into the room.
   – You've grown, Ben says to him.

– You always say that.

– It's always true.

– And you've grown smaller, Robert says.

– Robert, his mother says.

– That's how it is, Ben says. For a while we grow bigger and bigger and then we grow smaller and smaller.

– Why doesn't Dad grow smaller and smaller?

– He does, but you don't notice it because you see him all the time.

– I ought to notice it more if I see him all the time.

– It doesn't work like that, Ben says. It all happens in such minute stages that you don't notice if you see someone every day.

– What's minute?

– Tiny.

– Then why not say tiny?

– Because minute is smaller than tiny.

– Then why did you say tiny?

– Because it's the nearest equivalent.

– What's equivalent?

– When two things are alike.

– Then why not say alike?

– If you two have finished, his mother says, we can eat. They sit down at the table in the kitchen.

– How do you spell minute? Robert asks him.

– Like minute.

– Like minute?

– Uhuh.

– Then why is it pronounced mineyoot?

– Because that's how it is.

– But why is it like that?

– Please, dear, his mother says.

– And if they're written the same then how can you tell which is which when you see them written?

– You can tell from the context, Ben says.

– What's context?

– Robert, his mother says.

– What's context, Mum?

– What surrounds things, Ben says.

– How surrounds things?

– Enough, his father says.

– He's pulling my leg.

– I'm not, Ben says.

– Hurry up, his mother says. Everyone's finished their soup.

– Ben hasn't.

– You haven't given him a chance.

– Then everyone hasn't.

– They quarrelled all the time, Rick says.

– Did you? she asks him.

He shrugs.

– You're impossible, she says.

– There's nothing like a trip abroad by car to make a relationship fall apart, Ben says. Or cement it, of course.

– Cement it? Robert says.

– Don't interrupt, his mother says.

– Cement it? Like cement?

– Robert, his father says.

– I don't know why you went, Francesca says. You were already quarrelling like fishwives before you left.

– You know, Ben says, I've never heard fishwives quarrel. But then I don't know many fishwives.

– Like cement? Robert says.

– Robert, his father says.

– Besides, Ben says, I never quarrel. I'm not the quarrelling type.

– That's what's so infuriating about you, Francesca
says.

She gets up and clears away the soup plates.

– You know, Ben says to Rick, that card couldn't really
give you any idea.

– It looked pretty spectacular, Rick says.

– If you saw the real thing, Ben says. When you go out
on to the terrace after dinner, no matter how often you've
seen it, you still can't believe it. The whole valley's in
darkness with just a few lights dotting the hills and then
this, somewhere up in –

– You told me, Rick says.

– I'm telling Fran, Ben says. It's five or six miles away
but it seems to tower right up above you. Not threaten-
ingly, like Mont Blanc at Chamonix, for instance, but
somehow gently. Because of the way the rock glows. It
doesn't feel massive. It's just...

Francesca puts a dish down on the table, removes her
oven-gloves.

– Robert? she says.

– I don't want any.

– Why not?

– I just don't.

– You don't even know what it is.

– It's fish pie.

– You love fish pie.

– I'm not hungry.

– Of course you are.

– I'm not.

– Aren't you feeling well?

– No.

– What's the matter? Do you think you have a temperature?

– I'm not not feeling well.

– Don't be silly.

– I'm not hungry.

– You'll eat what you're given.

– Leave him alone, Rick says. If he doesn't want any he won't have any. But you're not eating anything else, he says.

– Here, Francesca says, have a bit of purée.

– Has it touched the fish?

– What do you mean has it touched the fish?

– I don't want to eat it if it's touched the fish.

– Don't be tiresome, his mother says. You know you like purée.

– I'm not hungry.

– You see, Ben says, that's what's so fantastic about the Dolomites. It's not like the rest of the Alps. The rocks are what make it so special. And it's not like rock in Britain. Even in the daytime it sort of glows.

– Like a glowworm? Robert asks.

– Eat, his mother says.

– Yes, Ben says. Just like a glowworm. A huge glowworm rising high up above you, ready to pounce.

– Cor! Robert says.

– Shut up and eat, his mother says.

– Is it really? Robert asks. Like a huge glowworm rising up into the sky?

– No, Ben says. Not really.

– Then why did you say it was?

– I said it glowed, that's all.

– No you didn't. You said it –

– Robert, his father says.

– I don't want any more.

– Aren't you feeling well? his mother asks.

– I just don't want any more.

– You're not getting up from table till you've eaten what's on your plate.

– Oh, Dad!

– Just eat what you can, his mother says.

– I have. I don't want any more.

Francesca gets up, fetches the oven-gloves, carries the dish to the sink.

Ben gets up, takes Rick's plate and places it on his forearm.

– Oh Dad! Robert says.

– Come on, his father says.

Ben stands beside Francesca at the sink, holding Rick's plate and his own.

– Put them down, she says, clearing a space.

– What's the matter? Rick asks his son.

– I don't want to eat.

– What've you got against fish all of a sudden?

– I just don't like the taste.

– Are you relieved? Francesca asks Ben at the sink.

– Mightily.

– She's not going to come back?

– No.

– Ah well, she says.

* * *

They are having coffee in the other room when the daughter comes in.

– Hi, she says.

– Hi, Ben says.

She kisses her mother and father.

– Want anything to eat? her mother asks her.

– No thanks.

– You've eaten?

– Uhuh.

– In that awful place? her brother asks her.

– Mind your own business.

– With those awful people?

– Coffee? her mother asks.

– No thanks.

– She doesn't have coffee any more! her father and brother chant together. Coffee is bad for the sys-tem!

– Oh shut up.

– Will you take Em out before you go to bed? her father asks her.

– Can I go too? Robert asks.

– No. You're going to bed.

– Oh Dad, please!

– Come on, his mother says. Don't be a nuisance.

– Can I take him out tomorrow night?

– You can take him out in the morning if you get up in time, his father says.

– No. I want to take him out in the evening.

– In the morning or not at all.

– Oh Dad! Why is Vee allowed to take him out and not me?

– Because she's older than you.

– Oh Mum, please!

– Come on, Francesca says. Bed.

– Oh, Mum!

– Do what your mother says, Rick says. Tomorrow we'll take him out together if you get up in time.

– Say goodnight, his mother says.

– Goodnight, Ben says.

Mother and son go upstairs.

Veronica crawls under the table and puts her arms round the dog, who thumps his tail on the carpet in response.

Rick stands in front of the fireplace, stirring his coffee. Ben, sunk in his chair, sips his.

– Something with it? Rick asks him.

– No thanks.

– Sure?

– I'm still feeling a bit fragile.

Veronica crawls out from under the table. She takes her bag from the sofa and leaves the room.

Rick puts his cup down on the mantelpiece.

– You know, Ben says, there was an Englishwoman at the hotel.

– I thought the English didn't go there?

– They don't. That's why it was a surprise that woman being there.

– I thought you only got Germans and Austrians in knickerbockers and a few Italians picking mushrooms.

– Sure, Ben says. Any more coffee left?

– Help yourself.

– She wasn't exactly English, Ben says, pouring from the jug.

– Oh?

– Her mother's family came from Constantinople.

– Istanbul.

– Istanbul.

– Turkish?

– No, no, Ben says, returning to his seat. Jews.

– And her father?

– Oh, English. She was born here.

He stirs the cream and sugar into his cup.

– And so? Rick says.

– So?

– What about her?

– It was just surprising, Ben says. That she should be there.

The dog crawls out from under the table and, with a deep sigh, stretches himself out on the carpet at Rick's feet.

– She was quite interesting actually, Ben says.

Rick prods the dog with the tip of his shoe.

– It's funny in these places, Ben says. You know. Like a ship.

– A ship?

The dog rolls over and looks reproachfully up at Rick.

– No, Rick says. No one's taking you out yet, you brute.

– We talked quite a bit, Ben says. We did that walk together.

– What walk?

The dog's tail, seemingly quite independent of his body, begins to thump again on the carpet.

– The one I told you about, Ben says. Round those seven peaks.

– She went all the way round?

– Oh she was a much better walker than me, Ben says. She was really used to those mountains.

– No, Rick says to the dog. Quiet.

The dog sighs heavily again.

– She could read maps and things at a glance, Ben says.

– Anyone can read maps, Rick says.

– Not contours, Ben says. Not to gauge the heights of passes and things.

– Anyone can master that, Rick says.

– Lily, Ben says.

– Lily?

– That was her name.

– Lily?

– From Liliane. After her grandmother.

– Liliane? Rick says.

– Why not?

– I don't know, Rick says. It just seems funny.

– Plenty of people are called Liliane, Ben says.

– I haven't come across any, Rick says.

– Not in England, Ben says. But in France and...all over the place.

He gets up and puts his empty cup down on the table, returns to his seat.

– She'd just come from Siena, he says. She'd been spending some time there before coming up to the mountains.

– On her own?

– Why shouldn't she be on her own?

– I don't know, Rick says. It isn't that usual.

– You're living in the nineteenth century, Ben says.

– It was unthinkable in the nineteenth century, Rick says. Today it's just unusual.

– Well I don't see anything unusual about it, Ben says. She went to look at a garden, he says.

– How do you mean a garden? Rick says.

28

– A hotel garden, Ben says. She went out specially to see it.

– I don't get it, Rick says.

– She wanted to understand how she came to be who she was, Ben says.

– What has a garden got to do with it?

– It was because of that garden that she was there at all.

– Where?

– Alive.

– Alive? Rick says. How do you mean?

– Well, it's difficult to explain. It was important in her grandmother's life. She wanted to try and understand how and why.

– What's that got to do with her being alive?

– Well, engendered then, Ben says.

– Engendered? Rick says. Engendered?

Francesca comes back into the room.

– Finished? she asks them.

– Thanks.

She starts to remove the coffee things. The dog gets up, stretching carefully, front legs first, then back. He yawns loudly.

– Not yet, boy, Rick says. Not yet.

The dog yawns again, looking into the distance, then turns round twice on the spot and eases himself onto the floor. He sighs.

Ben looks at his watch.

– I ought to be getting along.

– Have a drink before you go.

– No thanks.

He gets up. The dog does not move but watches him with care.

– I really ought to go.

He wanders into the kitchen.

– I've got to go, he says to Francesca.

– Already?

– I've still got some sleep to catch up on.

– It's nice to have you back, she says, standing on tip-toe and kissing him.

– It's nice to be back.

The dog is at the front door, wagging his tail.

– Not yet, boy, Rick says. Not yet.

He pushes the dog aside and he and Ben slip out. He closes the door behind him and they stand together on the steps.

– Well, Rick says. See you.

– Yes, Ben says. Thanks for the meal.

He starts off down the path. Rick eases himself through the door, gently pushing the dog back into the house as he does so.

* * *

In bed Rick says to Francesca: – He met some woman in the mountains.

– Is that what it was about? she says.

– What what was about?

– The quarrel with Sand.

– I don't think so, he says.

He puts out the light on his side. She does the same on hers. The beam from the street-lamp cuts across the ceiling where the curtains fail to join.

– What sort of a woman? she says after a while.

30

– From Istanbul.

– A Turk?

– No, no. A Jew. From England.

– I thought you said Istanbul.

– I did. Her mother's family came from there, apparently.

– I see, she says.

– Liliane.

– What?

– That's her name. After her grandmother.

– Liliane?

– That's what he said. Lily.

– Lily?

– There was something about why she was engendered and a garden, he says.

– What?

– Something to do with her grandmother.

– What?

– That's what he said.

– He didn't explain?

– Not exactly, no. She went to Siena to see a garden.

– Ben was in Siena?

– No no. He met her in the mountains. She'd come from Siena.

– You think he's fallen for her? she asks.

– He didn't say.

– If he talked about her he's thinking about her, she says. If he's thinking about her he's fallen for her.

– I don't see how you can say that, he says.

– That's how it is with him, she says. He meets them and then he thinks about them and then he thinks he can't live without them and then when he's lived with them for a while he realizes it was all a mistake and can't wait to see them disappear.

– Oh come on! Rick says.

– I'm only repeating what you always say.

– I never said that.

– More or less, she says.

After a while he says: – He only mentioned her because we'd run out of topics to talk about.

– He doesn't know his own mind, she says.

– I don't think that's fair.

– Well he doesn't, does he?

– Does anyone?

– I love you when you get philosophical to protect him, she says.

– I'm not getting philosophical and I'm not protecting him, he says. It's typical of the way you argue.

– I'm not arguing, she says. I merely made an observation.

– Anyway, he says, there's nothing to protect him *from*.

– Did I say there was?

– I thought you did.

– I hope he takes up with her, she says. I merely observed that he doesn't know his own mind.

– I don't know what that means, he says.

– Yes you do, she says.

After a while she says: – Did he say what she was like?

– Like?

– Was she pretty?

– You have the mind of a romantic novelist, he says.

– What if I have? Aren't I often right?

– Fifty per cent of the time, he says.

– Well that's a high percentage, she says.

– He didn't even say what age she was or if she was married or anything, he says.

– If he talked about her he's thinking about her, she says. If he's thinking about her –

– Oh come on! he says.

– Just wait and see.

– There's nothing to wait *for*, he says.

– You'll see, she says.

After a while she says: – Did Em do all he had to do?

– I didn't ask.

– You must tell Vee not to rush him round the block. There's no point in taking him out if she doesn't give him a chance, is there?

– Oh I'm sure she gave him a chance, he says, yawning.

– Oh well, she says, if he needs to go out in the middle of the night it's you who's taking him.

– Don't worry, he says. He'll sleep like a log. We tired him out this afternoon.

– Where did you go?

– The windmill.

– Many people?

– No, he says. Hardly a soul.

– Well, she says, let's hope for the best.

III Absalom

It was in the bar of the hotel, immediately after dinner on the second evening of their stay in the mountains, that he had found himself standing next to the English-woman. He had nodded and smiled, then tried to make the girl behind the bar understand what he wanted.

– Two mint teas, he said in Italian. The girl looked puzzled so he repeated it in English.

– Tea? the girl said.

– Mint tea. For two.

The woman said something to the girl in German and the girl replied with a long string of words, then dived below the level of the counter.

– She's going to see if they have any, the woman said to him in English.

– Thank you, he said. Then, as they waited for the girl to reappear: – Won't you join us?

– Oh? the woman said. Are you sure?

– Of course.

The barman came across and said something to them in German. The woman replied.

– What is it? Ben said.

– We should go and sit down, she said. They'll bring it.

She followed him to one of the polished wooden tables by a window. He pulled out a chair for her.

– I'm Lily, she said, holding out her hand.

– I'm Ben. He shook her hand.

Sandra joined them.

– This is Sandra, he said.

– I'm Lily. She held out her hand.

– You had the key, Sandra said to Ben.

– Oh God.

The waitress arrived with her tray.

– It's all right, Sandra said. I went down to Reception and got the master.

– I'm sorry.

– I should have remembered.

– No, no. My fault.

Sandra sat down and drew her glass towards her.

– This doesn't look like tea, she said. It looks like hot water.

– The tea-bag's there, Lily said, pointing to a saucer.

– God, Sandra said. I always forget.

She split open the containing envelope, took out the tea-bag on its thread, lowered it into her glass.

– Look, she said. Nothing happens.

– You must press it against the edge with your spoon, Lily said.

– God, Sandra said. You'd think no one had ever heard of tea in this country.

She took her spoon and did as Lily suggested.

– The water's tepid, she said. How can you expect anything to happen?

– You've been here long? Ben asked Lily.

– A few days.

– We arrived yesterday.

– I know, she said. I saw you.

– This is ridiculous, Sandra said.

– You did? Ben said.

– I was on the terrace. Across the road.

– How long are you staying?

– I haven't made up my mind yet.

– We've got a week, Ben said.

Sandra took the dripping tea-bag out of her glass and dropped it in the ashtray. A trail of water attested to the transfer.

– God, Sandra said. What a mess!

– You're English? Ben asked the woman.

– Yes.

– We are too.

– I know.

He laughed, embarrassed.

– Not many English people come here, she said.

– I know, Ben said. I found this place quite by accident last year, driving back from Verona.

– Do you like it? Lily asked Sandra.

– To be honest, Sandra said, I haven't been feeling too good since we arrived.

– Is it your first time in the mountains?

– More or less.

– It's the altitude, Lily said. One soon gets used to it. But it's silly to do too much at first.

– I hope you're right, Sandra said.

– Sand works for the Egg Marketing Board, Ben said.

– Really?

– I'm a teacher. And you?

– I'm not anything.

Sandra made a face.

– Did you order mint tea? she asked Ben.

– Isn't that what you wanted?

– It doesn't taste like mint to me.

– Oh?

– It's more like camomile.

Ben busied himself with his tea-bag.

– Ugh, Sandra said. I hate camomile.

Ben bent over his glass and sipped, eyes closed.

– You may be right, he said, straightening.

– You're sure you asked for mint?

– Lily helped me out.

– It's definitely camomile.

– They're not used to herb teas here, Lily said.

– But if one asks for mint…?

– I'm sure they'll bring you mint if you say.

Sandra pushed her glass away.

– Ugh, she said, grimacing.

– They probably got the bags mixed up, Lily said. I'll ask them to change it.

– It doesn't matter, Sandra said.

– It's no trouble.

– No, no. I've already drunk half of it.

– What was yours? Ben asked Lily. Cappuccino?

– That they're good at, she said laughing.

A group of very fat Austrians at the next table had got out a pack of cards. One of the women shuffled expertly and dealt the cards out fast, avoiding the bottles and glasses.

Five young men in full Tyrolean costume entered and made straight for the bar. They crowded round it, laughing loudly and exchanging banter with the young waitress.

– Don't they have any comfortable chairs here? Sandra asked.

– They don't seem to go in for them in this part of the world, Lily said. They expect you either to sit up on hard wooden chairs and drink or lie on your bed and sleep.

– I think I'll opt for the bed then, Sandra said.

– You're sure you're all right? Ben asked her.

She pushed back her chair and stood up.

– Of course.

– I'll be up soon, he said.

She held out her hand.

– The key.

– Oh. I'm sorry.

– Goodnight, she said to Lily.

– It's the air, Lily said. It's so rarefied up here one feels funny at first.

– I certainly feel funny, Sandra said.

They watched her make her way through the crowded café.

– I hope it's only the air, Ben said.

– It's the altitude, Lily said. Everybody feels it to some extent. After a day or two you adjust.

– She hasn't been feeling well for some time, Ben said.

– The altitude doesn't help.

– She's pretty tough, Ben said. I'm the one who usually gets the colds and funny tummys and things.

– It's different here.

He watched the card-players at the next table.

Lily made a gesture as if to gather up her things.

– Can I get you another cappuccino? he asked her.

– Thank you.

– And a cake?

She laughed.

– Go on, he said. Have one.

– You sound like my mother.

– Do I?

– I won't, thank you, she said. Just a coffee.

He called the waitress over. Lily ordered in German.

– I take it you want another mint tea?

– Yes. That's right.

The waitress made a long speech.

– She says she may well have mixed up the camomile and the mint, Lily said. Not many people ask for them.

He smiled at the waitress to show her it didn't matter.
– It doesn't matter, he said. I prefer mint though. If they have it.

The girl went away. He glanced at Lily's book, which was lying between them on the table.

– Only a guidebook, she said.

– You're going to Siena?

– I've just been.

– Really?

– Uhuh.

– Was it hot?

– Baking.

The waitress returned with their orders.

– You're an art historian? he asked Lily as he took the tea-bag out of its envelope and dropped it into the glass of hot water.

– I told you, she said laughing. I'm not anything.

– Nothing at all?

– What do you want me to be?

– No I just...

– Nothing at all, she said, spooning up the cream.

He sipped his tea.

– That's better, he said.

– The other was definitely camomile?

– I'm afraid so.

She stirred the cream and chocolate into her coffee.

– You're interested in art though? he said.

– Quite.

– But it's not the art you went for?

– No.

– And it's too late for the Palio.

She burst out laughing.

– What is it? he asked her.

– So many questions.

– I'm sorry.

He drank some more tea.

– Much nicer, he said.

– Why didn't you say straight away?

– I'm not very good at spotting things like that. I don't think my taste-buds are very highly developed.

She laughed again.

– How long were you there? he asked her.

– In Siena?

– Uhuh.

– A week or so.

She drank down her coffee and wiped her lips carefully with the paper napkin.

– We came straight here, he said.

– From England?

– We drove down through Germany and over the Brenner.

– How did you find this place?

– The hotel you mean?

– The hotel. The valley.

– I told you. I came up this way from Verona last year and just turned off and stopped at a place at the bottom of the valley. It made me want to come back, so this year I persuaded Sand to come and we drove up the valley and came to this place.

– You're lucky they had rooms.

– You've been before?

– Yes. People tend to come back.

– I'm not surprised. They know how to look after you.

The bar was crowded now. Another group of card-players had installed themselves on the other side of them, talking loudly as they splashed wine into their glasses.

He said: – What did you like best in Siena?

– You mean the town or the art?

– Both.

– Those two little landscapes, she said. You know the ones?

He nodded: – Uhuh.

– They're supposed to be the earliest, aren't they?

– I think so.

– I like the one with the boat and the city wall best, I think, she said.

– And the Duccios?

– Of course, she said. But less than the little landscapes. I liked the way they seemed to be very precise renderings

41

of what the artist had seen and also quite mysterious. Because of the greens, I think.

– You know Siena well?

– I'd never been there before.

He finished his tea and pushed the glass away from him.

– I liked the train journey too, she said. Winding up through the hills from Florence. I liked that.

– And the piazza? he said. And the cathedral?

– Yes. Of course.

– And the mosaic in the cathedral? he said. On the floor there?

– Oh yes, she said.

– Absalom caught by the hair.

– Oh yes, she said.

– I've never been there when the whole floor's uncovered, he said. Apparently they uncover it for a week or two every year, that's all. I must find out when and go.

She put the guide-book away in her bag.

– They need to keep it covered to preserve it, apparently, he said.

They watched the card-players at the next table.

– Do you know what the rabbis say about Absalom? she asked him.

– The rabbis?

– Absalom gloried in his hair – therefore he was hanged by his hair, she said.

– Really?

– You remember how he used to cut off his mass of beautiful hair every year and weigh it in front of the people? To impress them. And to put pressure on his father David. Getting the people to follow him rather than David.

42

– I've never really read the Bible much, he said.

– You should, she said. It's full of good stories.

He rubbed a spot on the polished table.

– I wonder if it's really like that, she said.

– Like what?

– He gloried in his hair so he was hanged by his hair.

– You mean…?

– If life has a pattern like that. And, if it does, whether we can ever grasp what the pattern is when we're in the middle of it.

She looked straight at him. He lowered his gaze.

– I don't know, he said, rubbing at the spot on the table.

– Do you think Absalom understood? she asked him. At the end? In the wood?

He looked up at her again. She was still staring straight at him.

– I don't think he did, she said. I think he was tired and frightened and everything happened too fast.

She stood up abruptly.

– I have to go, she said. I need all the sleep I can get up here.

He pushed back his chair and stood up too.

– Goodnight, she said, holding out her hand.

He shook hands with her.

– Goodnight.

He watched her go, then sat down again and made a sign to the waitress. When she came he pointed to his glass and made a gesture which he hoped would convey to her that he wanted another glass of mint tea.

IV The Book

The next day it was raining.

– Oh God, Sandra said. What is there to do here when it rains?

– It may clear, Ben said.

But the girl at the desk was not hopeful.

– The clouds are covering the mountain. It is bad.

– It's not going to clear at all today?

– Who knows?

There was no sign of Lily at breakfast.

– It doesn't look too bad, Ben said, standing at the tall windows in the still empty dining-room. And up in the mountains it somehow isn't as wet as down below.

– I'm not walking in that, Sandra said.

– There's a church in the next village we could walk to, Ben said. It's about twenty minutes. It seems to have one of those painted wooden screens they go in for around here.

He read out what the guide-book said.

– 'The polychrome altar, in style gothic, with its fresh

and bright colours, executed by Hans Hocker of Brixen, disciple of Michael Pacher. Painted on back is four scene from life of St Valentine: St Valentine in before judges; St Valentine healing a sick; St Valentine in the prison; martyrdom of St Valentine.' I think it's definitely stopped raining, he said.

But it hadn't.

When they got back, damp and restive, the girl at the desk said: – Tomorrow it's good weather.

– You're sure?

– It's good weather.

They studied the barometer in the hall. It indicated that the weather was perfect.

– You see, he said. The rain never lasts in the mountains.

– But it says it's perfect weather now.

– It must be tomorrow, he said.

– Barometers don't forecast, she said. It must be broken.

He looked towards the girl at the desk and she nodded.

– It's broken?

– Always.

– I told you so, Sandra said.

* * *

Lily was at her table at dinner and they nodded to her and smiled. But she wasn't in the bar afterwards.

They sat down at the same table as the previous evening – they always seemed to be among the first to finish dinner – and ordered mint teas.

– Bloody hell, Sandra said when the little waitress had put the glasses in front of them.

Ben pointed to the tea-bag in the saucer.

– Christ, Sandra said.

When they had removed the envelopes and dropped the bags in the water and pressed them down with their spoons against the side of the glass and taken them out and dumped them in the ashtray, leaving the inevitable trail of water on the table, Sandra tasted her drink and said: – At least it's mint.

The bar was emptier than the previous evening. The landlord moved round, drawing the curtains, but though he stopped to chat in German to the people who had settled at the next table he merely smiled at Sandra and moved on.

Ben spread out the map between them.

– Why can't they just put the bags in when the water's boiling? Sandra said. I really can't understand them.

– It's a question of culture, Ben said.

– What's culture got to do with it?

– Different cultures, Ben said. Like butter and oil.

– I'm not talking about Tibet, Sandra said. I'm talking about Italy, for God's sake.

– Who said anything about Tibet?

– You did.

– I did?

– The only people I know who put butter in their tea are the Tibetans, Sandra said. I never heard of Italians doing so.

– I didn't say anything about putting butter in tea, Ben said.

– You didn't?

– Of course not. I'm not mad.

– Then I must be going deaf.

– Look, he said, moving the map across the table. We could try to get to this hut here. Then we could come down by this path and make it a circular walk.

– Actually, Sandra said, I don't feel too bad. Perhaps what I need is a good walk.

– We could start early and have lunch up there, Ben said.

– How high do you reckon that is?

– Two one five oh, he said, reading off the map.

– Metres?

– Of course.

– I feel terrific all of a sudden, Sandra said. I really feel like a big walk.

– You're probably getting used to the mountain air, he said. Lily said it would take a day or two.

On their way up to their room she took the stairs two at a time.

– Look at me, she said. I'm flying.

But the next morning she complained of a tickling in her throat.

– I don't think I'll come down to breakfast, she said. I feel terrible.

– Make an effort, he said. It may ease off if you get up.

She came down with him, coughing and spluttering, her eyes red and swollen.

– Oh God, she said. I feel awful.

– See how it goes after a cup of coffee.

He went across to the tall windows and looked out. The little waitress from the bar brought them their coffee.

– It's a beautiful day, he said, returning to the table. The girl at the desk was right.

– I am beginning to feel indescribably awful, Sandra said.

– It's the change of altitude, he said. Your system's probably still adjusting.

– It's going about it in a funny way, she said. Oh God! she said, sneezing.

He buttered his roll, studying the map.

– You go, she said. I'm spending the day in bed.

– No, no. We'll go tomorrow.

– What good's it going to do me if you stay here? she said.

– You might need things.

– Don't be silly.

– No, he said. I'll stay. I might take a little walk in the afternoon.

– Suit yourself, she said. But I don't want you to stay and then resent me for keeping you from your mountains.

– They're not my mountains. Anyway, I wouldn't mind sitting on the terrace and taking things easy today.

– Suit yourself, she said. I'm going to bed.

– You may feel better later on.

– I doubt it.

– Everything's exaggerated up here, he said. You feel much worse and then you recover much more quickly. You'll see.

– I can vouch for the first part of that, she said.

– Look how well you felt last night.

– It must have been the start of this.

– You said you felt fantastic. You looked well.

– It wasn't natural, she said. I can see that now.

– Shouldn't you eat something? he asked her.

– No. I feel awful.

– Stuff a cold and starve a fever.

– I feel awful.

– Try.

– I don't want to. I don't feel hungry.

– That's why it says stuff. Push it down. You'll feel better.

– Oh for God's sake!

– Sorry.

She blew her nose loudly.

– If you want to go up, he said.

– No. I'll wait for you.

She sneezed and blew her nose again.

– I'm going to need some more tissues, she said.

– I'll see what I can do.

At the desk the girl said: – You see? A beautiful day. Beautiful for walking.

– Thanks, Ben said. Is there a pharmacy in the village?

– Pardon?

– A pharmacy. Where you can buy tissues. For a cold.

– At the shop, the girl said.

– The self-service shop?

– At the shop, yes. They have for colds.

– Thanks, Ben said.

When he got back Sandra was lying fully clothed on the bed.

– I feel awful, she said.

– You want me to call a doctor?

– Of course not. It's just a common cold. But I feel awful.

– Why don't you undress and get into bed?

She sneezed again and blew her nose loudly.

– Well, Ben said, I think I'll go downstairs and read a bit. Do you need anything?

– Oh God, Sandra said. I feel awful.

– I'll tell them not to do the room, he said.

– Oh God, Sandra said. Why did I ever agree to come to this place?

* * *

Sitting under one of the big parasols on the terrace, trying, as he did on every holiday, to make some headway with *The Ambassadors*, Ben was surprised to see Lily coming out of the hotel. She looked round and he tried to catch her eye, but she did not seem to notice and turned and went into the bar at the side. A minute later she came out again and crossed the road to the terrace. He returned to his novel, but the scenery was too spectacular to allow him to concentrate for long. At the end of the valley, six or seven miles away, the great rock of the mountain stood out against the blue sky, its seven peaks leading the eye gently back along the ridge of pines to the green meadows on the other side of the valley. Occasionally, below, cars moved slowly up the newly-widened road to the village at the foot of the mountain.

A waiter came out of the bar and crossed the road to the terrace, bringing Lily a cup of coffee. Ben signalled to him and ordered a cappuccino. When it came he took his time over it, settled down to his book again, then shut it with a snap and got up.

He strolled over to her table.

– Hullo.

She smiled up at him.

– Sand isn't feeling too good, he said. We thought we'd take it easy today.

– It's nothing serious?

– No no. Just a common cold.

– Do you want to sit down?

She removed her things from a chair and he sat down.

– You're not walking today? he asked her.

She laughed.

– I mean, why aren't you?

She shrugged.

– Sorry. I didn't mean to be inquisitive.

– Do you want another cappuccino?

– Yes. I think I do.

– So do I.

She got up and went across to the bar.

– I'm sorry, he said again when she got back.

– What for?

– Oh…

She laughed.

– For intruding on you. For not going and ordering the coffee myself. For…

– For everything.

– Well…

She laughed again and he suddenly laughed too.

The waiter came out and brought them their cappuccinos. Ben pulled out a note and gave it to him. He counted the change and put it on the table.

– *Grazie*, Ben said.

– *Prego*, the waiter said, and left.

She said: – I'm learning not to be restless.

– Is it hard?

– For me, yes.

– Why?

– Why is it hard or why am I?

– Why are you?

– I don't know. It's my nature. It gets worse as I get older.

– Why not be restless? he said. If it comes naturally?

– I think it's bad.

– In general? Or for you?

– Oh for me. Only for me.

He shook the little packet of sugar till the contents had all settled into the bottom half, split open the top and poured it over the cream and chocolate.

– Why Siena? he said.

– Why Siena?

– I mean out of all the places...Or had you been everywhere else?

She laughed.

– I'm sorry I...

She laughed again.

– What is it? he said.

– What amuses me, she said, is the way you ask all these questions and then retreat apologizing as soon as I don't answer.

– I'm sorry.

She looked at him. He laughed.

– Seriously, he said. Why Siena?

– It's a long story.

– Oh?

She was silent.

– I'm sorry, he said.

She looked at him. He laughed.

The terrace had begun to fill with guests waiting to go in to lunch.

– I didn't mean to be inquisitive, he said.

– Oh there's nothing to hide, she said. It's just a long story.

– You don't want to tell me?

– I don't know if it would interest you.

– I'm sorry.

She laughed.

– Did you go because of your restlessness? he asked.

– Perhaps.

The church bell behind the hotel started to strike the hour. There was a rush for the dining-room by those assembled at the entrance.

– There are times, she said, when you feel you're going to burst if you don't do something. When it's as if you're at the crossroads of so many contradictory pressures you just can't stand it any more. Do you know what I mean?

– Yes, Ben said. I think so.

– That was one of those times, she said. I had to move or burst.

– And now?

– Now? she laughed. It's not so bad now.

She pushed her chair back and got up.

– I must go and put these things away before I go into lunch.

He stood up in turn.

– I'll see you later, he said.

– Yes, she said. That's right.

*   *   *

53

She was in the bar after dinner. He sat down at her table without asking and she said at once: – I saw you in San Cristofero this afternoon.

– Really? Where?

– In the churchyard. You were examining the tombs.

– You were there?

She laughed.

– I didn't see you.

– I was just above you. On the hill.

The card-players had taken up residence at the next table.

– Up there? he said. I didn't know one could get up there.

– It's a steep climb, she said. Not very long but very steep. You have to follow the north stream for a while and then turn sharp right and start to climb.

– I didn't see you.

– No, she said. You couldn't have.

– Amazing, he said. It seemed to be sheer rock.

– There's a bench up there. Almost on the edge. The rock falls away right at your feet. It's a good place to sit and look down the valley.

– You know the area well, he said.

– Moderately.

– You've been here often?

– Not often, no. I've come once or twice with my father and his family.

– His family?

– He has a young family.

– Your parents are divorced?

– Oh yes. Since a long time.

– I see, he said.

– My father likes to feel that everything's fine with the world, she said. He gathers people into groups and takes them off to exotic places. And he's good at it. He knows how to find the right places, organize things. He's the kind of man who hasn't been in a small Irish town for half an hour and he already knows who goes out fishing for fresh salmon and when the local dog-show is held.

– What does he do?

– He's a lawyer.

– And your mother?

– What about her?

– Does she do anything?

– She dreams.

– Ah, he said.

She sipped her coffee.

– How many half-brothers and sisters do you have? he asked her.

– One of each.

– I see.

– My father, she said, is the kind of man who goes through life pretending sadness and despair don't exist. Especially if he's the cause.

– You mean your mother?

– Not only her.

– You?

– No, no, she laughed.

The waitress brought his glass of tea. Lily said something to her and she laughed. She went away.

– Where did you learn your German? he asked her.

– I hardly have any.

– You seem able to get by.

– I went to a good school, she said.

As he dealt with the tea-bag he said: – And so your father comes here often.

– He used to, she said.

– Why used?

– He moves on. There are always new worlds to conquer.

– You see him much?

– No.

– And your mother?

– Occasionally.

– She didn't remarry?

– So many questions! she said.

– I'm sorry.

– No, she said. She didn't remarry.

He was silent, looking down into his glass.

– I'm going to have one of those cakes, she said. Do you want one?

– No thanks.

She got up and went over to the counter. When she was settled again he said: – You were close to your parents as a child?

– Oh...

She dug into the cake with her fork.

– I just...

– You see, she said, my father's a very successful man. His field is international law. Marine law. He's always flying off to advise companies and governments.

– Well, he said, it's –

– He wants everyone round him to be successful as well, she said. To be doing things. Succeeding. He's very jolly too, she said. And feels everyone ought to be jolly as well. Moping is bad. That sort of thing.

She finished her slice of cake, licked her fork and pushed the plate away from her.

– And your mother?

She looked at him.

– I'm sorry.

– What about?

– Well I...

She laughed.

– You get on with her?

– I get on with both of them. I'm not particularly fond of either.

– I see.

– I got on better with my grandmother than with either of them.

– She's dead?

– Yes.

He finished his tea and pushed the cup away from him.

– It's because of her I went to Siena, she said.

– Oh?

– Yes, she said.

He was silent, not wanting to look at her.

– What are you going to do tomorrow? she asked him.

– I don't know. It'll depend on Sand. And you?

– I might climb a peak I once did years ago.

– Which one?

She spread the map out on the table between them and showed him.

– I don't see a hut up there, he said.

She laughed.

– Am I looking at the wrong place?

– No.

– There seems to be nothing but rock.

– There's a path, she said, pointing.

– I don't see where it leads to.

– The top, she said. Only the top. Where there's a big wooden cross with a little box fixed half-way up the upright and a book inside the box.

– A book?

– Uhuh.

– I don't get it.

– That's what they do around here.

– Do?

– You're supposed to write your name and address in it. To show you've been there.

– Show who?

– Other people who get there I suppose.

– You wrote your name? The last time?

– I imagine so.

– You want to check?

She shrugged her shoulders.

– It doesn't look very inviting to me, he said, scanning the map.

– There are pretty good views.

– Is it sheer?

– On one side, yes.

– Then I'm afraid it's not for me, he said. I haven't got much of a head for heights. Not when it's a sheer drop.

– You don't have to look down.

– But one does, he said. You know how it is. Even from a third-floor window I find myself drawn to look down and then my legs go all soft and I have to make a real effort to turn away.

– A third-floor window?

– You can put my name in the book for me, he said.

– I couldn't, she said. Not if you hadn't been up there yourself.

– I didn't really want you to, he said.

He studied the map.

– Are there really lots of crosses all over these mountains? he asked her. Each with a box on it and a book in the box and your name in the book?

She laughed.

– While mere tourists like myself walk along the well-marked paths and stop at the huts and have a drink and never even know about these books?

He pulled the map towards him.

– I'll tell you what I'd like to do, he said. I'd like to go round the mountain. Right round the whole thing.

– That's a long walk.

– But there are plenty of stopping places. And it's not so high, is it?

She leaned over the map with him.

– It's pretty high over that pass there, she said.

– Would it take long? he asked her. Could I do it in a day?

– I don't know. I should think so. Seven or eight hours. Something like that. It would depend on your pace.

– I don't think Sand'd want to do it, he said. But it seems like *the* walk to do round here. Judging by the map.

– I've never done it, she said. Not all the way round. I don't know anyone who has.

– You obviously prefer to go upwards.

– It seems like the right direction, she said.

He examined the map: – Seven or eight hours you'd say?

– If you take the car to the bottom there.

– I might try, he said. Would you join me?

– It's a long walk.

– If one started early, he said.

She pulled the map towards her and bent over it.

– Come on, he said. It'll be a change for you.

– Sandra isn't a great walker?

– She's all right. I'm not sure she'd be up to that one though. Even if she recovers quickly.

She looked at her watch.

He called the waitress over and they paid.

They went out into the night.

He looked in the direction of the mountain but there was nothing to be seen.

– Did you see it after supper? he asked her.

– Of course. I always make a point of coming out and watching till the light drains out of it.

– You think it'll be fine tomorrow?

– Oh yes, she said. The weather's cleared now. It should be fine for a while.

– I was afraid we'd hit a bad patch.

– It's never bad for long here, she said. Not at this time of year.

– I'm going to walk down the road a bit, he said. Do you want to come?

– I don't think so, she said. I think I'll turn in.

– I'll see you in the morning then.

– Uhuh.

– Goodnight.

– Goodnight.

He stood watching her go back into the hotel, then started to walk down the steep hill leading out of the village. At the bottom, by the little round chapel, he stopped and looked back up the hill at the lights of the hotel and the few surrounding houses. He tried to pick out their room on the top floor, under the steep roof, wondering if Sandra was reading or had put out the light, but it was impossible to be sure which one it was.

He threw back his head, looking up into the blackness of the sky, breathing deeply. Then he began slowly to walk back up the hill.

V Things About Her

A few weeks later, as he sits in the kitchen in Putney, watching Francesca take the provisions out of her shopping bag, he says: – Do you think I should phone her?

– Why not?

– I don't even know if she's gone back there.

– But if that's the address she gave you?

– She hadn't finally decided what she was going to do, he says. But that's the only address she had. She said he'd forward things if she wasn't there any more.

Francesca puts the food away methodically, the bread in the bread-bin, the vegetables in the vegetable-rack, the butter and cheese in the fridge, the sugar and marmalade in the cupboard.

– Perhaps I should write and let him forward it, Ben says.

– Why not? she says. Take your arms off the table for a moment.

He holds his arms high while she passes a cloth over the pine surface.

– But then if she doesn't reply I won't know if he's forwarded my letter or not.

– You can put your arms down now.

– Will I?

– Will you what?

– Know if he's forwarded the letter or not.

– Then phone.

– I don't really like the phone, Ben says. Anyway, what should I say if he answers?

– Ask for her.

– I hate talking to people I can't see. It's even worse if I've never seen them.

– Then write.

– Do you think it's silly? he asks her.

She has her back to him as she washes the lettuce at the sink.

– Silly? she says.

– Of me.

– What is?

– All this.

– It's up to you, she says.

She wraps the loose lettuce-leaves in a tea-towel and goes past him and out into the little back garden. He watches her through the open door as she walks up and down, up and down, waving her arms.

– What was that about? he asks her as she comes back in.

– What?

– Who were you signalling to?

– Silly.

– Callisthenics?

She stands at the sink, her back to him.

– You won't tell me?

– I can't stand you when you're like that.

– Like what?

– Pretending to be silly.

– I'm not. You won't tell me?

– You've seen me do it before.

– No, he says. No.

– All right then, she says. Drying the salad.

– Why doesn't Rick get you one of those things that go round and round?

– I don't know. Ask him.

– Would you like me to get you one?

He stands beside her at the sink, picks up a carrot she has just washed and bites off the end.

– Don't do that, she says.

– Sorry.

– If you want to be useful peel the carrots.

– Where's the peeler?

– It's all right, she says. I'll do it.

– Just tell me where the peeler is.

– It's more trouble than doing it myself. Honestly.

– Telling me where it is is more trouble than doing it yourself?

– Yes.

– I don't believe you.

He finds the peeler and a stack of old newspapers. He spreads one of the papers out on the table.

– How many? he asks her.

– Do the ones I've washed.

– Will that be enough?

– There're lots of other things.

– Perhaps I'll try phoning all the same, he says, holding

a carrot up to the light and examining it. Like that I'll know if she's gone back to him even if she isn't in.

– Did she say she'd be in touch?

– No. You know how it is. One exchanges addresses and that's more or less that.

He starts to peel the carrots.

– You know, he says, if you're ever in the area give us a ring. As if I'd ever be in the area. It's practically Bromley.

– Of course, he says, he could just say he'll pass on the message and then not do anything.

– Write then, she says.

– He could throw the letter away.

– All her letters?

– Well, he could be feeling vindictive.

– I suppose he could.

He lays the peeled carrots alongside each other on the draining-board beside her, goes back to the table, rolls the newspaper with the peelings into a ball and drops it into the rubbish-bin.

– You can grate them now if you like, she says.

– Where do you keep the grater?

– There. Do it on a plate.

– It was the dog she really missed, he says. Bess. How do you want them grated?

– The large side, she says.

– I think it was really because of the dog she thought of going back, he says. Otherwise she wouldn't really have considered it, I think.

He chews the base of the carrot he has just grated.

– Do you really think it's silly of me? he asks her.

– What is?

– To want to get in touch.

– Why silly?

– I don't know. There are things about her I found terribly off-putting.

– Like what?

– I don't know. She wore little ear-rings all the time.

– Everybody wears ear-rings.

– I know. It just put me off. Even when she was dressed for climbing.

He hands her the plate of grated carrots.

– Anything else?

– Do the cucumbers if you like.

– I couldn't really get interested in her, he says. Sexually I mean. Not with those little ear-rings.

– Is that necessary?

– It depends.

He presses a slice of cucumber peel to his forehead and closes his eyes.

– Do you think that's what being mature means? he asks her.

– Mature?

– That you can overlook the sexual aspect?

– I wouldn't have thought so, she says.

– You mean one can't really overlook it? Ever?

– I don't think maturity has anything to do with that.

– Nothing at all?

He cuts the peeled cucumbers into slivers, carefully.

– Mature, he says. Responsible. Taking decisions. Weighing the pros and cons. It must be wonderful to be like that.

– Finished? she says.

– Uhuh.

He hands her the plate.

– I couldn't really understand, he says, whether she'd come to Italy because she was trying to leave this chap or because she needed to see that garden.

– Do you mind sitting down again? she says. You're in the way.

– Sorry.

He sits again.

– I couldn't understand if this crisis she talked about had to do with that chap and being with him, he says, or with something else.

– Didn't you say the dog?

– No no, he says. That was a side-issue.

– You said she –

– She just said if she hadn't got away she'd have choked. That was the word she used. Choked. The dog was just a side-issue.

– Why couldn't she leave the chap and take the dog?

– It was his dog.

– Ah, she says. I see.

– Anyway, he says, she felt she had to get to that garden. She had to sit in it and think things through.

She goes past him again and out into the garden. She comes back with a leaf of mint.

– Not that she realized that, he said. Till she got there.

– Where?

– To the garden.

– Realized what?

– That that's what she'd been after all the time.

– You've lost me, she said.

– Perhaps I should try to phone, he says.

She starts to make the dressing for the salad.

– Do you think I should?

– Go ahead.

– She may not even remember me.

– Then you can remind her.

– And then?

– How should I know? she says. You must have some idea of what you want to say to her.

– I suppose, he says, I'm curious to know whether she ever went back to him or not.

– Tell her that then.

– That I've just rung out of curiosity?

– If that's the truth.

He rubs at a spot on the table.

– No, he says finally. I couldn't do that.

– Then don't ring her up.

– Somehow, he says, I don't think she can have. Gone back to him I mean.

– And the dog?

– Yes, he says. She might have gone back for the dog.

– The only way to find out's by phoning, she says.

– Yes, he says. I suppose you're right. I wish I didn't hate the phone so much.

VI The Upper Meadows

They had set out from the hotel immediately after breakfast. The best time to walk is before lunch, Lily had said.
One has twice the energy before lunch as after.

The weather had settled. The sun shone from a cloud-
less sky but up in the mountains the air was cool. They
left the car at the car-park by the three cafés which
passed themselves off as *rifugi*. Though he had thought
they would be among the first and it was well past the
high season the car-park was already almost full. But
the giant mountain seemed able to absorb any number
of people and for a while, on the broad steep track
through the lower pinewoods, they were alone.

Lily walked fast and he had trouble at first keeping up
with her. The sun broke through the cover of pines and
down below them the valley shimmered.

A sound cracked through the trees.

– Guns? he asked her.

– No. The cowherds do it with their whips.

– They make them crack like that? Listen.

There it was, again and again.

– They do it just for fun, she said. And perhaps to impress the tourists.

Ahead of them a large group trudged up the steep track in silence. He was pleased to see how slow they were, how quickly the two of them were gaining ground.

– They're all so fat, he said under his breath as they caught up with them.

She laughed: – It's the beer.

– Everyone seems to be like that around here. Those red check shirts and huge stomachs bulging out of their knickerbockers. One wonders how they can get up these mountains.

– They'll tell you the beer helps.

– How can it? Look at them.

– That's what they say.

He had to make a constant slight effort to stay with her, but together they passed the straggling group, exchanging greetings as they did so.

– Those shirts don't help, he mumbled as they moved ahead.

– Help?

– Their figures.

– I don't think they're too concerned with their figures.

– I hope not, he said. There'd be a lot of unhappy people around if they were.

The cracks echoed round the great shell of the mountain.

– They really do sound like guns, he said. You're sure they don't go shooting here?

– It's a national park, she said. It's all protected. Anyway, no one would let off guns with all these hikers about.

70

He stopped at a bend in the track and looked back. The forest thinned on the slope of the mountain and he could see the meadows they had just left and tiny figures running about on them.

She was waiting for him at the next bend.

– The air's good, he said. It makes walking easy.

– Once you get acclimatized.

– Yes, he said. Sand kept getting out of breath. Even after a couple of minutes.

– She'll be all right in a day or two.

– She's decided already this isn't for her, he said.

They reached a signpost.

– That's the steep way, she said. We'll take the other.

He had a look at his map and was shocked to see how little they had done.

– Another half-hour, she said, and we'll reach the upper meadows. Then it levels off.

– I should get some knickerbockers, he said.

– It helps if the knees are free.

He was beginning to sweat now, and stopped to take off his pullover and put it away in his rucksack. When he looked up again there was no trace of her. The sweat poured off his forehead and into his eyes, but he shook his head and plodded on up the mountain.

He wondered now if it wouldn't have been better to have gone by himself. He resented her for going so fast. He wasn't enjoying it, pushing himself like that. She was ruining his day. He would have been better off staying with Sandra. However, he kept on after her, his eyes fixed on the ground a few feet ahead of him, and he was pleased to find that he was passing more and more people, most of them obviously hardened walkers too, with the inevitable knickerbockers and red check shirts.

The landscape had begun to change. The forest was starting to thin out and the dolomite was now visible above them through the trees.

She was standing at the next bend, looking up at the rocky mountain through her binoculars. She put them away as he drew level.

– Have an orange.

– Thanks.

They stood and ate while a single hiker, going fast, went past them.

– Not much further now.

– To the top?

She laughed: – No no. Just the upper meadows.

They trudged on. At every bend he expected to see the meadows but there was only more forest, and the path, if anything, grew steeper. The landscape was definitely changing though. Single pines now stood out by themselves in the midst of giant boulders, some even growing on top of these miniature mountains.

He willed himself on, planting one foot in front of the other and lifting his body forward up the side of the mountain. He had never been so conscious of gravity in his life, but he was determined not to show her how difficult he was finding it to keep up with her.

And then, round a bend, the wide concave shell of the upper meadows appeared, surrounded on three sides by sheer dolomite. To the left the meadows sloped upwards and in the distance he could make out a small group of buildings with a tiny hut perched precariously on top of a cliff almost directly above them.

The tinkle of cowbells came through the rarefied air

72

and he realized he had been hearing them for some time.

She was sitting on a rock waiting for him. He sank down beside her.

– Worth the climb, don't you think? she said.

He slowly took off his rucksack and set it on a rock between them. He unzipped the outer pocket, took out a bar of chocolate and offered her a piece.

– No thanks. Not for the moment.

A family, in jeans, the mother with what looked like a plastic shopping-bag in her hand, the father paunchy and balding, trudged towards them along the path. A young dalmatian, flanks gleaming, danced up to them. She patted his head and he sat down, looking at them expectantly with brown freckled eyes.

The man whistled to it and with one last sad look at them he trotted off.

– This is where I miss my dog, she said.

– You have a dog?

– Uhuh.

He put the remains of the chocolate away in his rucksack.

– I have friends who have a dog that grins, he said.

– Oh?

– Grimaces really. When he looks at you. I've never seen a dog do that. They call it Emil after Emil Zatopek, the great Czech runner.

– Why?

– He was a great grimacer. When he ran. Rick was a runner too. Zatopek was his idol.

– It's Frank's dog really, she said.

– Frank?

– The man I live with.

– Ah, he said. What kind of a dog is it?

– Oh, a mongrel. He got her from a home.

– What's she called?

– Bess. That's the name she had when he got her.

He sang: –   Come over the bourn Bess,

My little pretty Bess,

Come over the bourn to me.

– What's that?

– A song Shakespeare uses in *King Lear*.

– How does it go?

He sang again: –   Come over the bourn Bess,

My little pretty Bess,

Come over the bourn to me.

– I'll have to remember that, she said.

He zipped up his rucksack.

– I wish she was here.

– Yes, it's a good place for dogs.

– Better than South London.

She looked round at the mountains closing in on them from every side, then pointed: – That's what we're making for.

– You're joking.

– No I'm not.

– That there? Right up in the sky?

– It shouldn't take more than an hour. We'll have coffee there.

– How does one go?

– Oh, the path winds round. You'll see.

– It doesn't look possible.

– You'll see.

– All right.

– Are you ready?

– When you are.

– Let's go then.

Now the track merged with the meadows and he found he could keep up with her.

– The lower *rifugio* serves better coffee, she said. But it would leave us too much to do afterwards.

– You're the leader.

She laughed: – It's your walk.

– My walk?

– You thought of it. You persuaded me to join you.

– All right then. My walk. But you're my guide.

She set off. He bent down and rolled his jeans as far up as they would go, then ran and caught up with her:

– Am I holding you back terribly?

– Not at all. The secret in the mountains is to give yourself plenty of time and never rush.

– I see a crest, he said, and I feel I can't slow down till I've reached it.

– That's because you're not used to the mountains. Up here a crest doesn't mean anything because there's always a higher one behind it.

– Yes, he said. I'm beginning to realize that.

Now he could see that the silvery, big-eyed cows, more reminiscent of deer than of the English cows he was used to, were pasturing in the meadows round the group of houses. Children ran about between them, chasing each other and shouting. As they approached he realized that the terrace of one of the houses was teeming with hikers, sitting on benches and eating or staring up at the rocky mountain through binoculars.

She kept to the path, which wound round the houses

75

then left them at an angle and began to wind its way up the mountain. Though he put on a spurt he didn't seem able to cut down the distance between them any more. After a while he stopped to get his breath back. The houses were already a long way below them, the figures on the terrace and in the meadows as tiny as ants. He turned and went on climbing after her.

VII Floating

Later, in London, he was to say to Francesca: – That last bit of the first part of the walk was the real killer. The jeans pulled at my knees, the rucksack weighed on my back, and all these fat old people kept going past me up this endless dusty track which I couldn't even see properly because of all the sweat pouring into my eyes. At first, he says, I promised myself not to stop till I reached the top, just to go on putting one foot in front of the other till I got there, but then my heart was beating so hard and my legs felt so wobbly I just stopped. Like an overladen donkey. And went on when things had calmed down inside me, and stopped again when it all got bad again.

– For the first half hour or so, he says, I would look up at the hut above me whenever I stopped and try to measure the distance still to go. But after a while, what with the twistings and turnings of the track and the sweat in my eyes and the pain in my chest, I gave up doing even that. I just stopped caring. I wanted more than anything else to lie down and close my eyes but there were all these people on the path and it would have been too much of an effort to hunt for somewhere to lie down away from them all. So I trudged on, stopping more and more frequently and for longer and longer. Not sitting, just stopping where I stood, more and more frequently and for longer and longer. And then moving again, more and more slowly. And suddenly I was there. I had been imagining that moment for so long that it didn't register at first that this was real. There were all these people on the grass and on benches against the walls of the hut and at little tables dotted about on the grass and waiters in white aprons running to and fro carrying great plates of sausages and bread and huge mugs of beer and bowls of soup and trays piled with cold meats. I looked round for her and finally saw her on the grass with her back to a boulder, watching me as I came up the path.

– Coffee never tasted so good, he says. Or had such an immediate effect. I could feel every sip making its way down my throat and through my chest and down into my stomach. She gave me a piece of chocolate and I actually began to feel rather well. One of the things that kept amazing me in the mountains, he says, was how quickly I got tired and how quickly I picked up again. We've done all the climbing for the moment, she said. Now we reap the rewards.

– I went in and had a wash and then I was actually keen to get going again, he says to Francesca as they sit in the kitchen in Putney. We climbed the gentle slope towards a large group of signposts and as we did so the whole of the other side of the mountain came into view, with snow-covered peaks stretching on and on eastwards towards Yugoslavia and Austria. We were on a ridge and, looking back, we could see the great shell we'd just climbed, and then the valley beyond, in which, somewhere, stood the hotel from which we had set out that morning, and, at the end of that, cutting across it from north to south, the great range that separated us from Lake Garda and the Swiss Alps. Ahead of us was another circle of mountains. Here the land fell away much more abruptly and, far below, we could see a few clusters of houses and even a steeple through the morning haze. She pointed to where we had to go and we turned right, leaving the crowds behind us immediately.

– The path kept just east of the ridge, he says, so that the hut where we had had coffee was no longer visible. We were moving slowly round to the other side of the great dolomite. From this side it looked much less impressive, just a jagged outline with sparse grass growing in the lower crevasses and nothing but scree higher up with, here and there, lodged in the rocks above us, a few white patches, the only remains of the winter glaciers. We now started to climb again, he says, but across the mountain this time, rather than upwards. I was finding it easier, either because I had got into the swing of things and found my second wind, or because it was less steep. She kept ahead of me and didn't slow her pace, but I found I was able to keep up without too much effort. Once or twice the path crossed small patches of frozen snow which crunched beneath our feet but held firm. Though the sun was directly above us now it felt quite cold up there and I had to stop and put on my pullover. There were hardly any hikers and those we met were coming from the opposite direction. The families with the picnic baskets were well and truly behind us now. The people we encountered were in small groups with massive rucksacks on their backs and efficient-looking light-weight walking-sticks, expertly wielded.

– Then, he says, we found ourselves in a chimney and the path petered out amidst fallen stones and larger patches of frozen snow. I could feel a headache coming on and my legs felt like lead. She didn't seem to be affected by anything, just kept on climbing, and I swore I wouldn't call out to her to wait for me. We could see the opening above us, where the mountains parted and the sky showed through. There were people up there, he says, we could hear their voices, but the going was so difficult that it was necessary to concentrate on where you put your feet at every step or you risked sliding all the way down, so they remained nothing but disembodied voices.

– It must have taken us half an hour to climb that chimney, he says. Every joint in my body was screaming for me to stop, but somehow it wasn't mentally as bad as the first stretch, perhaps because I'd already done that and I knew I could do it again, and also because this was clearly a very tough stretch and I felt I had a right to be tired.

– Eventually, he says, we got there. One always does. The people we had heard up there earlier had vanished, and we looked down from the pass into another chimney, even narrower than the one up which we had just struggled. There was a cold wind blowing up there and the sun seemed to have got covered by a thin layer of cloud. It wasn't my idea of an idyllic picnic spot but when she suggested we sit and eat our lunch I suddenly realized how hungry I was. I could hardly get my rucksack open I was so desperate to get at the contents.

– This is the highest we go, she said, studying the map as she munched her sandwiches. You said that at the last stop, I said, but she rightly insisted that she hadn't actually said that. No more climbs then? I asked her. One more, she said. Here. Look. But I was happy to leave the map-reading to her. It's a hillock compared to what we've already done, she said. Nothing at all to worry about.

– Even with two pullovers and a windcheater on it was getting cold, so as soon as we'd eaten we set off again, down the other side. Actually, he says, the whole of this next stretch was a big disappointment. In one way it was good, it made me feel good that we were staying in the other valley and had that marvellous view all the time of the dolomite, sheer white rock reaching up into the sky, while the people in this valley had nothing but a series of very ordinary slopes covered with scrub and scree and not even a very clear outline of the seven peaks, since from here they all seemed to merge into one. The tree-line didn't seem to begin till several hundred feet below, even when we'd left the chimney and were striking parallel to the main mountain range. But the ground was soft, almost marshy, because of the many little streams cutting across our path.

– It was suddenly busy again here, he says, with families picnicking in the meadows and children playing in the streams. Though it was easy to walk side by side, he says, we didn't talk much. I think she was almost as tired as I was. We crossed a number of dried-up streams and went over several low hills, and then we were at another hut, a small one by itself in the middle of the sloping meadowland. For the last hour I'd been dreaming of another cup of coffee or perhaps two even, and I just sat there on a bench, in the shadow of the wooden wall and the overhanging roof, too tired to go and wash my face, dreaming of the sweetness of it and the warmth. When it came and I slit open the two packets of sugar and emptied in the contents – you know the way the sugar stays lying on top of the cream and the chocolate in those cappuccinos – I had lost any sense of whether this was actually happening or still part of my day-dream.

– We stayed there for a long time, he says. People were continually arriving and leaving and there were lots of children playing about, but we seemed to be floating in a world of our own, eating enormous cheese sandwiches and drinking that wonderful coffee. We talked, but inconsequentially, picking up a subject and then dropping it not because we had dealt with it but as if it was too much of an effort to hold on to anything for any length of time.

– And gradually, he says to Francesca in the kitchen of the house in Putney, it was as if my body, which had separated itself from me and had been walking and sitting and standing at a little distance from me, was returning, taking up its rightful place, piece by piece, until I could feel every bit of it, not in pain but with a warm glow of contentment.

– And so, he says, we set off for the last climb and the last pass and the last really steep descent, and then we were on the other side of the mountain again, and walking round it to where we had first climbed up. But on this side our path was firm, cut out of the rock, and led through the pine-trees, with the sight, every now and again, of the mountain rising high above us. I don't know about her, he says, but the feeling of well-being I had experienced in the last hut had long since gone and now there was only the sense that every step was taking us nearer and nearer to the car and home. It's not that I wasn't enjoying the view and the feeling of achievement, he says, but that they seemed to be experienced by someone else, someone connected to me but not in any meaningful way. I had been taking aspirin for my headache and I kept yawning and wanting to lie down on the side of the path and go to sleep, but I resisted the temptation and just kept putting one foot mechanically in front of the other. Not much more to go, she encouraged me, and I was too tired even to grin a response at her.

– Of course, he says, it took much longer than I had imagined. We still had a good two and a half hours of walking to do, with the occasional excruciating short climb, and it passed with a kind of nightmarish slowness. There were more people about again on these paths, and almost the worst thing was having to stop to let a group pass in the opposite direction, because the effort of starting again was so great. But finally we began the last descent. My feet were killing me by this time, and going down was agony. My toes seemed to be on fire and I sensed I had blisters on the soles of both feet. But now we could hear the tinkle of cowbells again and the cracks of the whips below us, and eventually, unbelievably, the car-park appeared through the trees.

– We had another cup of coffee down there, he says, on the terrace of one of the cafés, with a view up towards the hut where we had first stopped, it seemed like months before. The sun had come out again and we took off our boots and twiddled our toes in the breeze to see if there was still any life in them. We were both too tired to talk by then, and our faces hurt too much from all the sun and wind we'd had throughout the day, so that even opening our mouths was painful. My feet weren't actually in as bad a shape as I'd feared, only sore, and it wasn't too pleasant putting the boots on again. But I'd left some sandals in the car and all we had to do was hobble a couple of hundred yards to get to it. The car-park was still quite full, though it was getting on for seven o'clock. I didn't know how well I'd be able to drive along those narrow winding roads back to the hotel, but, very slowly, we made it.

– Sand was waiting on the terrace, he says to Francesca in the kitchen in Putney. She seemed to have perked up since I'd left her that morning. I didn't feel much like going in to dinner but decided I'd better make an effort. And in fact when the food arrived I found I was quite hungry. But tired as I'd never been tired in my life. Sand was telling me what she'd done during the day and I kept nodding and making the appropriate noises, but I wasn't taking any of it in. Afterwards she wanted to go to the bar and I thought I owed it to her to go along, but the moment I stood up I knew all I was good for was bed. I climbed the stairs in a sort of dream and got into the room somehow and sat on the bed and started to take off my clothes. I don't know why but I was extra careful folding them and putting them away, although I kept messing it up and having to start again. But eventually it was done and I lay down on the bed – very slowly too, as if I was afraid if I made any violent movement it would collapse under me. When I was completely stretched out

I just let go of everything and had a sense of sleep like a great wind rushing towards me, and then I was out. I didn't even hear Sand come in and get into bed beside me.

VIII   In the Garden

The day after the great walk Sandra announced that she
was going shopping in Bolzano.

   – Do you mind if I don't come with you? he asked her.

   – Why should I mind? You do what you like, don't you?

   – I mean I'd come tomorrow but today all I want to do
is rest.

   – Well I rested yesterday, she said. Today I want to go
and do some shopping.

   – Do you mind if I don't come?

   – You've asked me that already.

   – Sorry.

   – That's if you don't want the car.

   – Why should I want the car?

   – I don't know, she said. You had it all day yesterday.
I thought you might want it again today.

   – No, he said, I don't want it. Anyway, it's your turn to
have it.

   – That's what I thought, she said.

   – I might come with you if you go in the afternoon.

   – No. I want to go this morning.

– Fair enough.

Later, in the kitchen in Putney, Francesca is to say to him: – You can't blame her for feeling a bit sore, can you?

– Who's blaming her?

– You sounded a bit peeved.

– I didn't mean to.

– It doesn't seem to me she was having much of a time, Francesca says.

– No, he says. She wasn't.

– I just thought you might try to see her point of view.

– I do, he says. I did. The trouble was it never seemed to coincide with mine.

– I must confess I always did find her a bit difficult, Francesca says.

– You did? Why didn't you say?

– Say?

– I always thought you liked her.

– I did, quite.

– I always thought you got on with her.

– I did. But there were times when I could have slapped her.

– You mean when she said you coddled Robert?

– It wasn't any of her business.

– Well, he says, she was always outspoken.

– You can say that again, Francesca says.

– She always meant well though.

– I'm sure she did. But it wasn't any of her business.
He is silent.

– Perhaps it was a mistake to go to the mountains, Francesca says.

– It was her idea.

– You'd been urging her for ages.

– All right, he says, it was my fault.

– I didn't say that.

– I thought that's what you were implying.

– I wasn't implying anything. I was just asking you to see her point of view.

– All right, he says. All right. Perhaps it's me. Perhaps I lack commitment.

– Perhaps, she says.

– I don't know.

– How can you?

– How can I?

– Not you. I mean one.

– I feel I do, he says. But then I find it hard to know what one should commit oneself *to*.

– Yes, she says.

– Don't say yes like that.

– How do you want me to say it?

– I don't know.

– I suppose, he says after a while, when there aren't any children to hold you together there comes a time when there just doesn't seem any reason to stay together.

– I suppose so, she says.

– But it's probably me, he says. I lack commitment.

But that was in the future. In the mountains that morning after the great walk Sandra drove off to shop in Bolzano and he lay on the bed and dozed after breakfast till the maid came round to do the room.

– Oh, she said, peering in at him, *scusi*!

– It's all right, he said. I'll be out of the room in a moment.

* * *

It was already hot on the terrace and she had opened up one of the big parasols that stood on concrete pedestals between the tables.

– Good morning, he said.

She smiled up at him: – Feeling sore?

– Not really, he said. Just splendidly lazy.

– I know, she said. I do too. Do you want to sit down?

– I don't want to disturb you.

She laughed.

– Why do you laugh?

– You're so English. You apologize all the time and then say things like that.

– Well I don't. If you're busy.

– Do I look busy?

– You might want to be alone.

– Then I wouldn't have asked you to sit down.

– You might have felt…

– What?

– I was going to say felt you had to. Then I realized you wouldn't feel that.

– You've lost me, she said.

The waiter crossed the road to take their orders.

– Cappuccino for me, she said.

– Two please, he said.

– You slept well? he asked her when the waiter had gone.

– Like a log.

– So did I. I didn't think I would, I was so tired.

She laughed.

– You're not going to tell me about that garden? he asked her.

– Garden?

– In Siena.

– It's a long story.

– We have time.

– I'm not sure I want to go into it.

The waiter brought them their coffee.

– Why you went, he said.

– I told you, she said. I'm not sure I want to.

He waited, watching her.

She spooned up the cream and chocolate from her cup.
He waited, watching her.

She wiped her lips with the paper napkin and sat back
in her chair.

He waited.

She looked at him.

– Shall I tell you about the man in the hotel? she asked
him.

– If you like.

– I kept hearing this typewriter in the afternoons, she
said. Through the open window. When I was trying to
rest. Day after day. Non-stop. And then one evening, in
the garden, there was this man at the next table, and we
began to talk. He was American. He worked for the New
York City police force. Apparently these police officers
in New York have to read Henry James before they let
them out onto the streets. And Wordsworth.

– Oh yes?

– I'm not joking. At least they have to read some books
and learn how to write. That's what he told me anyway.

– He was a policeman?

– I don't know. I suppose he must have been. His job
was to teach them about literature.

– He found it rewarding?

She laughed.

– Anyway, she said, he told me he finished teaching in May and came straight out to Italy. He always booked a room in the same hotel and spent the summer there writing. He told me he was writing a historical novel about Siena. It was a big project, he said. A long-term project. He kept using the phrase, a long-term project. At the end of every summer he went back to New York and taught these policemen for another year. Then in May back he would come to the hotel. He was on his third draft, he told me.

Some of the guests were strolling up and down the road between the hotel and the terrace. Others stood at the edge of the terrace, looking down at the car-park and chatting to those setting off for their morning excursions.

– He told me, she said, that he'd started by staying in Florence, but he didn't like Florence any more. It had grown too busy. There were too many tourists. You couldn't move for tourists now, he said. And besides, it was too expensive. He couldn't afford to stay there for the whole summer, not on his teacher's salary. And he needed to do that if he was going to get on with his book. It takes a month to unwind, he told me, a month before I can put a single sentence down on paper. And then another month before I can construct a sentence that really satisfies me. After that, he said, it's plain sailing. I can keep going all day. After that, he said, it's a question not so much of whether I can write but of how I can restrain myself.

The terrace had emptied. Only the two of them sat there drinking coffee and talking.

– What was it about? he asked.

– Siena and Florence in the Middle Ages, she said.

– Ah.

– About the rivalry between the two cities. He had to do a lot of research, she said. He was still reading masses of background material. He read in the mornings and took notes, he told me, and then in the afternoon and evenings he wrote. Like that he hoped to finish the third draft by the end of the following summer.

– He showed you some of it?

– No.

– So you've no idea what it was like?

– No.

– But he was an interesting man?

– Not very, she said, and laughed.

– I didn't get to know him, she said. You know how it is. One talks about quite intimate things between tables, like that, in a hotel garden, and then it's as if one had never really talked at all. We nodded to each other after that, when we met on the stairs or in the dining-room or in town, but we didn't really talk again. I think he may have been embarrassed that he'd said so much that first day.

– But you know his name. You'll look out for the book.

She laughed.

– What...?

– If I hear of a novel about Siena in the Middle Ages I'll read it, she said.

– Then you can write him a fan letter.

– Somehow I don't think it'll be my sort of book, she said.

A car came up the hill, its radio blaring. It screeched to a halt in front of the hotel and a young man leapt out, slamming the door, and hurried into the bar. The radio, in the empty car, blared on.

– My God, Ben said.

The man came out of the bar, jumped into the car, started up the engine, did a violent U-turn and tore off down the hill. The sound of car and radio gradually died away.

– I suspect he won't ever get it finished, she said.

She turned her chair a little and looked down the valley.

– But that's not what you went to Siena for, he said.

She laughed.

He waited, watching her.

– You're waiting for me to tell you, she said.

– Uhuh.

– I'm not sure why I went, she said. In order to try and understand I think.

– Understand what?

– Oh...

– And...?

– What?

– You did?

– Understand?

– Uhuh.

– I don't know, she said.

He waited, watching her.

Finally she said: – Part of it has to do with stones and trees I suppose.

– Oh?

– Trees in stony places.

He waited.

– Siena, she said, is a stony city. Set on top of a stony hill. When the sun is high there is no shade at all. No shelter from it. As you know.

– Yes, he said.

– But on the edge of the town there are gardens, she said. Facing out towards the surrounding hills. There's a hotel on the west side of the town, she said, whose façade gives on to a stony square, but you go in and on the other side, facing the hills, there's a large garden with trees and paths and little overgrown alleys. It's not really very big, as gardens go, but for Siena it's immense. And it's intricate. You can't exactly get lost in it, but you can't hold it in your head either.

She stopped.

He spooned up the froth from the bottom of his cup and licked the spoon.

– You only have to walk a few steps and you reach a wall, she said. A parapet really. From there you can look down the hill at the road winding up from the valley below. The hill is covered with little vegetable plots. Dozens of them, all neatly tended, with row upon row of different vegetables and vines and olive trees too.

– The parapet curves, she said, following the line of the hill. Wherever you are, if you look down you see these little plots.

– Once you lose sight of the house, she said, it's difficult to tell exactly where it is any more. Because everything curves and the pines cut out your view. One can't imagine, she said, from the square, that there could be such tall and leafy trees in a place so dominated by stones.

– So much, she said, for the garden.

She was silent.

– Was that where you met your writer? he asked.

– Policeman, she said.

– Policeman.

94

She was silent, gazing down the valley.

– You'd been there before? he asked her.

– No.

– Then…?

– My grandmother had told me about it.

– She'd been there?

– As a young woman, yes.

– Why did she tell you about it?

– Something happened in that garden, she said. Something happened to her. Before she was married.

He waited.

When she remained silent he said: – It hadn't changed?

– I don't know, she said. I don't think so. I recognized it at once. From the way she had talked about it.

– What had happened to her? he asked.

– It was very peculiar, she said, arriving there and finding it really existed.

– You went in order to find it?

– I don't know, she said.

– How do you mean?

– I didn't admit it to myself, she said. Not when I booked the flight to Florence and not when I took the plane and not even when I got on the train for Siena, not even when I arrived there. But I suppose I was really looking for it.

– Why?

– That's what I'm trying to explain.

He waited.

– Somehow, she said, it shouldn't have been there. It belonged in a story my grandmother told me. It was very peculiar, finding it there, part of an ordinary hotel you could book into like any other. I still find that difficult to make sense of, she said.

95

She was silent.

– Your mother's mother? he said.

– Yes. I'm called after her.

– You got on with her.

– Much better than with my parents. I felt I had more in common with her than with them. Always.

– Why?

– I don't know. I think I felt from early on that they were drifters. Life just happened to them. Not that my father doesn't work hard. He does everything flat out. But he doesn't seem to think about things. To feel things. And my mother's just given up.

– But not your grandmother?

– I don't know how to explain it, she said.

– She lived with you?

– No. By herself. In a village near Oxford. She was a very independent old lady. She loved the English countryside. Rather unusual for a Levantine Jew, but she did. She'd had an English nanny when she was small and England had always been a dream for her.

He waited.

– She never tried to tell me how to lead my life, she said.

– And your parents did?

– Yes.

He waited.

– Didn't yours? she asked.

– They never showed much interest in me.

– You're lucky.

– Am I? I always thought not.

He shifted his chair so as to have the sun at his back.

– Especially my mother, she said. My father was too

busy with his family. But he made a point of telling me
what he thought I should be doing.

– And what did he think you should be doing?

– Getting married and having children.

– I see.

– Failing that, I should have a serious job.

– You didn't satisfy him on either count?

– No,

He waited.

– My friend Frank, she said. The one with the dog. He
was keen for us to marry too. That's partly why I came
to Italy.

– To escape?

– To try and think things through.

– And?

– What?

– Did you?

She laughed.

– What conclusion have you reached? he asked her.

– None, she said. Of course.

He waited.

– I had to get away, she said. I had to be by myself. To
try and understand.

– Understand what?

– Everything.

– Everything?

She was silent.

– And the garden? he said.

– That seemed to be at the heart of it, she said.

He waited.

– You see, she said, I just felt I had to get away and so
I went and bought a ticket and took a plane and then a

train and I got out in Siena and wandered around in the heat for a bit carrying my stuff and feeling it getting heavier and heavier and then I came to a square and a hotel, just an ordinary building in a stony square, but it said hotel and I looked through the glass doors and all of a sudden I knew.

– Knew what?

– When you looked through those doors, she said, you looked straight through a sort of foyer thing and out into a garden beyond.

He waited.

– I peered through the doors, she said, and it was there and I knew suddenly that I had really been expecting it all the time.

He waited.

– All the way from Florence, she said, in that little train, we'd been going through stony hills. And then Siena itself seemed to be made of nothing but stone. Not a tree in sight. I wasn't even thinking of trees. I'd forgotten there were such things as trees. And then walking about the town with my bags, not really knowing what I was doing and the day getting hotter and hotter. And then this.

– But it wasn't the trees, she said. It was the whole thing. I knew at once it was the garden she'd talked about. And I knew why I'd come.

– I suppose after the first shock I thought it must be an illusion, she said. A *trompe-l'oeil* painting on the back wall. Something like that. Or plants inside the foyer. It didn't seem possible to have all that green actually exist-ing and growing outside. Not in Siena. And it didn't really seem possible that it was the same garden. Things like that just don't happen.

The waiter came out to serve a couple who had settled at the further end of the terrace.

– Another coffee? he asked her.

– Please.

They waited in silence for the waiter to return with their orders. When he had done so and left again she said: – I pushed the door open and went in. I needed to find a hotel anyway. And I wanted to see. My first impression had been more or less correct. It was a garden I was looking at, though it was further away than I had thought, because you had to walk not only through the foyer but also through one end of the dining-room to get to it. And it wasn't quite as cool and shady as I'd imagined from the street because the glass was tinted and outside everything was a little drier and the trees a little dustier than I'd at first imagined. But it was still a kind of miracle. I dropped my bags at the desk and crossed the foyer, which was empty, and the dining-room, where the tables were already laid for lunch, with lots of silver glinting and crisp napkins rising in little spirals from the plates, and out through the doors and straight to the parapet. I leaned against it, she said, and looked down.

She shook her head as if to clear it and said: – You don't want to hear all this, do you?

– I asked you, he said.

– The first day, she said, they gave me a room on the square at the front. It was the only room they had free. They said it was the best room in the hotel. It may have been. It was enormous. The bed alone was the size of most rooms I was used to. There were four free-standing pillars in it, holding up the ceiling, whether they were structural or not I don't know, but they added to the strangeness, and the ceiling was certainly a long way up. When the woman first showed it to me it was so dark I couldn't see a thing, and felt my way over to the windows and threw them open, and the shutters too. That let in the light, but it also let in the noise. I hadn't realized when I was in it that that square was so busy. It seemed to be filled with lorries revving up and mopeds racing through from one side alley to another, the way Italian mopeds always seem to do under your hotel windows.

– In Siena? he said.

– We were on the outskirts of the city, she said. Just outside the city gates. So traffic could get there. And it did. I asked if there wasn't even a tiny room at the back but she shook her head. It was all they had available and it was the best room in the hotel anyway and no more expensive than the others. However, she admitted when she saw my face, a very small room at the back, without bath or shower, would be available in two days' time, so if I stayed I could have that.

– And you did, he said.

– Of course I did, she said. I hardly slept a wink for those two nights. With the windows shut the heat was unbearable and with them open you felt you were right out there in the middle of the square. I got to the point where, if there was a silence for a few seconds, I'd start to get anxious and wake up completely, listening, waiting, and only start to relax again when, far away in the distance, I heard again the sound of a moped approaching or a lorry changing gear as it crawled up the hill.

–But I stuck it out, she said, and after two nights they gave me that room at the back. No bath or shower but a blessed silence. And the sight of the garden. Just the sound of the crickets at night. I'd thought I'd still hear the lorries coming up the hill, but the angle must have been different or something and when one did hear them they sounded very far away. So I slept, she said. For a long long time.

– And then, he said, you heard the sound of typing.

– Yes, she said. In the afternoons.

– And then you met the writer.

– Policeman.

– Policeman.

She was silent.

– You told him about the garden? he said at last. Why you'd come?

– No.

– No?

– There was nothing to tell. And anyway he was too taken up with his novel. I was just someone he happened to get into conversation with one evening. He'd probably talked to most of the guests at one time or another during his stay. We were part of the furniture.

She was silent.

He waited.

– I miss my dog, she said.

– Bess?

– Uhuh.

He sang: –   Come over the bourn, Bess,
                    My pretty little Bess,
                    Come over the bourn to me.

She was silent, looking down at her empty cup.

– You'll be back with her soon, he said.

– I may not go back.

– To England?

101

– No, no. To Frank. And Bess.

He waited.

– You could get another dog, he said.

– I don't want another dog. I want Bess.

– Of course.

– But I had to get away, she said. Everything was sort of pressing in on me. Choking me.

– It happens, he said.

– I didn't expect it to happen to me.

– No, he said. One doesn't.

– I was quite happy, she said. With Frank. And Bess. I'm probably still quite happy with them. But at the same time I was choking.

– Everybody needs a break, he said.

– I didn't mean that.

– I'm sorry.

She laughed.

– You needed to see that garden? he said.

– Yes.

– And now?

– Now?

– It's made a difference, seeing it?

– Yes, she said.

Cars were beginning to draw in to the parking-place beneath the terrace. The guests were starting to gather at the hotel doors, waiting for the lunch-gong to sound.

– What did she tell you? he asked her. Your grand-mother?

– It's a long story.

– You won't tell me?

– I don't know that it would make much sense to any-one else.

– You could try and see.

– I am trying, she said. It isn't easy.

He was silent.

– I have to get ready for lunch, she said.

– Yes, he said.

The church bell behind the hotel started to ring out the hour. As it finished the lunch-gong sounded.

– I have to go, she said, getting up.

– Yes, he said. Me too. I'll see you later.

– Yes, she said.

* * *

In his room after lunch he lay down on the bed and tried to sleep, but there was too much light in the room. He got up to close the shutters, then decided to go and sit out on the balcony instead.

He adjusted the heavy wooden deck-chair and stretched himself out, gazing at the mountain range across the valley, taking in the different shades of green as the conifers gave way to the meadows and these descended in gentle humps to the little river gleaming below.

He got out his notebook and tried to sketch the view, but the perspectives kept eluding him. He stood up and leaned on the balustrade, looking down into the little apple orchard below, dotted with garden tables and chairs.

He put away his notebook and went downstairs. He walked round the side of the house and emerged at the edge of the orchard.

He made his way through the apple-trees till he was standing at her table.

103

– Hullo, he said.

– Hullo.

– I'm not disturbing you?

– Sit down.

– Are you sure?

She laughed.

– I wasn't sure it was you, with the sunglasses on.

She took them off.

– I didn't mean…

– I'll move my chair. I hate talking to people with them on.

He looked round him.

– I hadn't realized this was here.

– There's even a gym, she said, pointing. And a sauna.

– Goodness. Who uses them?

– Me.

He laughed.

– I don't know anyone else who does, she said.

– Well well well. One lives and learns.

She smiled at him.

– Every day? he asked her.

– Every day what?

– You use them every day?

– No no. Once in a while. When it's raining. People tend to make use of it more in winter.

– You've been here in the winter?

– Yes. It's lovely.

– Do you ski?

– Cross-country, she said. That's the beauty of this valley. It's not equipped for the other kind so it stays quiet through the winter.

He waited, watching the crickets at his feet. Then

he said: – You were going to tell me about that garden.

– So I was.

He waited, watching her.

She fiddled with the glasses on the table. Finally she said: – I don't know how to tell it.

He closed his eyes, stretching his legs out in front of him.

– I realized as soon as I first mentioned it to you that I didn't know how to tell it, she said.

He opened his eyes and looked past her down the valley.

– It's just one of those things that makes no particular sense in itself, she said. It just gathers meaning in time, for the people involved.

He turned a little and looked at her. She remained leaning forward, playing with the glasses on the table.

– It was probably a mistake, she said.

– What was?

– Mentioning it to you.

– You must have felt it would help.

– I wanted to hear it, she said.

– And you don't any more?

– I don't know, she said.

He waited.

– I tried this morning, she said. I didn't get very far.

He waited, watching her.

– All this makes it sound much more interesting than it probably is, she said.

– Everything can be interesting, he said.

– Not other people's dreams.

– But this isn't a dream, is it?

– No. But it's not that different. I realized when I tried to tell it. Like a particularly vivid dream that leaves you with a strong feeling afterwards but there seems to be no way from the feeling to any account that will convey why it feels like that. And so of course the feeling gradually fades. Because it has nothing to hold on to.

He waited.

– You see, she said, it's as if I will only make it make sense to me if I can tell someone about it, but when I start just the opposite happens and it turns into something trivial.

He waited.

– You probably don't understand what I'm talking about, she said.

– Oh…

He waited.

– Don't tell me if you'd rather not, he said. We can talk about something else. Or not talk at all.

– On the walk, she said. When we were really tired. Coming down on the other side. And then sitting having coffee in the hut. I had the feeling that I was telling you about it and it was making sense – to me and to you. I didn't need to find the words, they were just there, I had only to think them and you heard them. Not even think them. Do you know what I mean?

He shook his head.

– We were so tired, she said. It was as if we were turned inside out. Do you understand? Like gloves.

He laughed.

– But of course I wasn't talking at all, she said. We were both of us much too tired to talk.

He waited.

Finally she said: – The trouble is, there's nothing much to it.

– Why not say that nothing much?

– Because of all this preamble. You're expecting some

extraordinary revelation. And the more I go on like this
the more you expect.

– No, he said.

– Aren't you? Tell me the truth.

– Perhaps, he said.

– You see.

She was silent.

– Why not tell it as though there was nothing to tell,
he said. As though it was dead.

She was silent.

– As though it had nothing to do with you.

She was silent.

– Then perhaps you'll discover what it does have to do
with, he said.

She was silent.

– You can't not tell it now, he said.

– No, she said.

He waited.

She said: – I didn't know why I was going and I knew.
When I saw the garden through the doors of the hotel I
knew at once that that was what I'd really come for. But
now I'm confused again.

– Since coming here?

– No, she said. After that first moment. It was all clear
in that moment and then it grew confused again.

– How confused? he said.

– When I looked through those doors, she said, I knew
at once that this was the garden she'd talked about and
I knew I'd really come to find it and now I'd found it
everything was resolved. Then I wasn't sure any more.

He waited.

She put the sunglasses on, took them off again.

She said: – My grandmother would often talk to me about a garden. In Italy. *The garden in Italy*, she would say. I don't know how I imagined it. The word *garden* took on a kind of magic for me. The words *hotel garden*. The words *garden in Italy. The garden*, she would say. *The hotel garden.*

– I can't remember when she first told me what happened in that garden, she said. I don't think she told me in any connected way. She always spoke about it as though I knew already. As though we'd been there together. *When I left the garden*, she would say. *We sat in the garden*, she would say. *We sat there for a long time and then it was time for him to go and he went. It was very quiet in the garden*, she would say. *Nobody disturbed us. We talked about all sorts of things*, she would say. *We talked about everything. Nobody disturbed us. It was as if we were sealed off from time. And from other people. It was as if I was there with him, talking*, she would say, *and as if at the same time I was at an upstairs window, looking down at us talking. I couldn't hear what we were saying but I could hear our two voices, like two streams, intermingling and flowing together. And then it was time for him to go*, she would say, *and he went.*

– *I sat in the garden for a long time after he went*, she would say, she said. *And it was as if the two streams were still flowing, glinting in the light as they flowed over the stones, now together, now apart. As if they would go on flowing like that for ever, as streams do, in the sunlight, in the shade.*

She was silent.

He waited, looking down the valley at the mountains in the hazy distance.

– The way it happened, I think, was this, she said. They used to go to Italy every summer. When they were young. She and her sister. With their parents. They would sail from Constantinople on one of the cargo ships which regularly made the rounds of the Eastern Mediterranean ports: Alexandria, Haifa, Ephesus, Constantinople, Athens, Venice. Sometimes they had the chance to get off and explore. That was how she first saw the Acropolis. There were hardly any tourists in those days, she said. You climbed up by yourself to that gleaming temple. She had never been back but she had never forgotten it.

– When they got to Venice, she said, her father would always book them into the same hotel, and they would spend a few days there before going to the mountains. Sightseeing. Getting acclimatized. He was a great believer in doing things in an orderly fashion. Then they would take a train for the mountains. They usually stayed not far from here. By the lake of Carezza. Her father was convinced that everyone needed a dose of mountain air at least once a year. He'd made friends with other families who were also regular visitors. There were games of tennis and dances for the young people, and trips up into the mountains.

– One year, she said, there was a family there who hadn't been before. A woman from Trieste and her two sons and the wife of one of the sons. The other son was waiting for his fiancée to arrive. They met at a dance and got talking. When the young men discovered that my grandmother's family came from Constantinople they asked her if she knew of anyone with a certain name who lived there, distant relatives of theirs whom they'd never met, only heard of. But that's our name, said my grandmother. Then we're related, they said.

– It wasn't all that surprising, she said. Jewish families from that part of the world had spread all over the Eastern Mediterranean. And as they didn't own land they had memories instead, and genealogies, as Jews have always had.

– Anyway, she said, because of that coincidence and because they got on so well they spent much of that holiday together, my grandmother and her sister and the two young men and the wife, and the parents with the mother. My grandmother told me that when she was in Italy as a young woman, she said, she found to her surprise that whenever she got on really well with people they nearly always turned out to be Jews. This was all the more surprising because Italian Jews have Italian names and are more or less totally assimilated. But there it was. She thought perhaps it had something to do with there being a sense of something more complicated, older somehow, in the Jews than in the Italians, to which she found herself responding.

She stopped.

He waited for her to go on.

After a time, when she showed no sign of doing so, he said: – And then?

– In the evenings they danced, she said. And in the daytime they went for long walks up into the mountains. But still the fiancée didn't show up.

She stopped again.

– Where is it exactly? he asked.

– What?

– This lake.

– Over there, she said pointing. Due south. About fifty

kilometres away. The mountains are beautiful there too. Almost as beautiful as here.

He waited.

– They're called Rosengarten in German, she said. Much more beautiful for once than the Italian name, which is Catenaccio.

– Meaning what?

– Padlock, she said. There is a legend that the Sleeping Beauty was shut up in those rose mountains, till the knight came and rescued her.

He waited.

– It really is like a garden of roses, she said. When the sun shines on the rocks.

– Why didn't you go there?

– I tried it once, she said. But I hated it. Now it's all ski-lifts and hotels and yet also somehow desolate. I didn't like it at all. But it must have been different then.

He waited.

– Anyway, she said, the days passed and the fiancée still hadn't turned up. No one mentioned the fact but everyone was thinking about it. The young man didn't seem too upset though. He and my grandmother were together a lot. They were better walkers than the others, and better dancers. And the fact that they were distantly related made things easy between them.

She was silent again.

– Anyway, she said after a while, the time came eventually for my grandmother's family to leave.

She stopped again. He watched the crickets jumping in the grass at his feet. Down the valley, in the meadows, the farmers and their wives were cutting the hay.

– It seems, she said, that they were booked to spend a

111

few days in Siena. Their father had decided to take them on a short tour of central Italy, and they stopped at Pisa and then went on to a hotel in Siena. After that they would go to Florence and then back to Venice to catch the boat for Constantinople.

She stopped. He tried in his mind to draw the sweeping contours of the coniferous slopes across the valley as they merged into each other in the blue haze.

– So, she said, they said goodbye and went down to Pisa and then Siena, and they stopped at this hotel.

– The one you went to?

– Yes. The one with the garden.

He waited for her to go on.

– On the third day of their stay, she said, the young man arrived.

– They were expecting him?

– No, she said. They'd said goodbye in the mountains. And now there he was.

He waited.

– He had left his parents and brother and sister-in-law up there, she said, and followed my grandmother and her family to Siena. He had dinner with them that evening, and the next day she found herself alone in the garden with him.

He waited, but she was silent.

– Yes? he said, after a while.

– They sat there and talked, she said. They talked right through the day, sitting in that hotel garden. No one disturbed them. It was so quiet in that garden, she told me. Nobody disturbed you. Even the sun, because of the trees, left you alone.

He waited.

112

– That was when she felt their two voices were like two streams, she said. When she felt she was there with him, in the garden, and also somewhere above, looking down on them talking.

– What did they talk about? he asked her.

– Everything, she said.

He waited.

Eventually she said: – He told her he had to leave the next day, she said. He was going back to Trieste to continue his musical studies. He was a violinist at the conservatory there. He asked her if he could write to her and she said yes. He asked her to let him know the date of her arrival in Italy the following year and he said he would come and meet her at the boat. Then he had dinner with the family and the next morning when they came down to breakfast he was gone.

– Nobody commented on the oddity of his turning up in that hotel in Siena like that, she said. It was as if it was too important to talk about casually. So they went back to Constantinople and she began to correspond with him. Her sister got engaged that year, and then married. On the day of the marriage a letter arrived from him saying that he too was getting married, to the girl who hadn't turned up in the mountains.

She was silent.

– What did she do? he asked her.

– She didn't reply, of course, she said.

She was silent.

– And then? he said.

– He kept sending her letters, she said, asking how she was. She didn't reply. And then one day he sent her a little toy donkey that moved its head up and down when

113

you twiddled its tail. You know the kind.

– I don't understand, he said.

She was silent.

Then she said: – She was furious. She thought he was laughing at her.

– And then? he said.

– Then nothing for a long time. They went away again that summer, just herself and her parents, and they went to Carezza again, but the family wasn't there.

– And then? he said.

– Then?

– What happened?

– He wrote again, asking if she'd received the donkey. She didn't reply to that either.

He waited.

– The following year, she said, she met my grandfather and he proposed to her and she accepted him and she had my mother and then a few years later her husband died.

She was silent again.

– And then? he said.

– Then time went by and my mother grew up and the war came and they escaped to Egypt where they had relatives and my mother met this English officer and married him and after the war they all came over to England.

A cricket jumped onto his lap and immediately jumped off again.

After a while he said: – What are you trying to say?

– I don't know.

He waited.

– Why did you feel you had to go there? he said.

– To the garden?

– Yes.

– It seemed important.

– Why?

– I don't know.

He waited.

– Why did you feel the need to talk about it? he asked her.

– I don't know.

He turned his chair a little and looked at her. She was playing again with the glasses on the table between them.

– You said this morning that when you saw the garden through the doors of the hotel it was like coming home, he said.

– Yes.

– What did you mean?

– As if I'd known it all my life, she said. As if at last everything was going to come clear.

– For you?

– I don't know how to explain it.

– Try, he said.

– I have, she said.

– I still don't understand.

– As if it was where I came from, she said. As if once I entered that garden I would know who I was.

– I don't understand.

– It doesn't matter, she said.

– Where you came from? he said.

– Why I'm me. Not someone else.

– That doesn't make sense, he said. I could see if she'd married him that...

– Yes, she said.

– Well?

– Yes, she said again.

– It doesn't make sense.

– No.

– Well then.

She was silent.

After a while he said: – If you thought there was even the possibility that he…that you…?

She laughed.

– Why do you laugh?

– No, no, she said. People didn't. Not in those families. Anyway, there wasn't…And my mother was only born two years later.

– Then why do you…?

– I don't know.

He looked down the valley at the farmers working in the fields below them.

– Thank you for listening, she said.

– I don't…

She put on the dark glasses.

– I don't understand anything, he said. I don't understand about the donkey or what they…

She was silent. He looked at her. He didn't recognize her with the glasses on.

– I must go and change, she said. It's getting chilly.

She stood up.

– I'm still…

– Thank you for listening, she said again.

– Thank you for telling me.

She shrugged, then turned and walked quickly away through the apple-trees and round the corner of the building.

IX   Lots of People

Walking up Putney Hill with Rick and the dog, Ben says:
– I tried to phone this morning.
  – I was in all the time.
  – No no. Phone Lily.
  – Lily who?
  – The woman I told you about. From the Dolomites.
  – Sit! Rick says.
The dog looks up at him pleadingly.
  – Sit!
The dog, still looking at him, lowers his behind a few
inches.
  – Go on, Rick says. Sit!
The dog sighs, lowers his behind a little further.
  – Now! Rick says.
Once across the road he lets the dog go and he disap-
pears into the bushes in a cloud of dust.
  – Go on, Rick says to his friend.
  – I just said I tried to phone her.
  – And what happened?

– Happened?

– When you phoned.

– I got the chap.

– Oh? Rick says. He whistles for the dog, who comes scurrying out of the bushes, his nose close to the ground, crosses their path and disappears again on the other side.

– I thought you weren't going to phone her, Rick says. Isn't that what you'd decided?

– Yes, Ben says.

Rick stops and whistles. Nothing happens. They begin to walk again, in the direction of the pond.

– What made you change your mind? Rick asks him after a while.

– I don't know.

– And so, Rick says. What happened?

– He went off to call her, Ben says. Then came back and said she didn't seem to be around.

– So?

– I think she may not be there any more.

– But if he went to call her?

– He could have been pretending.

– Pretending what?

– To call.

– You mean for your benefit?

– I had the feeling there was nobody there.

– But why shouldn't he just say so?

– I don't know, Ben says. I just had the feeling.

The dog is suddenly at their heels. Ben pats his head and the dog licks his hand, leaving a web of saliva over his fingers.

– Do you think I should try again? he asks, bending to rub his hand on the dog's coat.

– What made you change your mind? Rick asks, as they enter the underpass.

– In what way?

– I thought you weren't going to phone her.

– I don't know, Ben says.

They emerge and head for the pond.

– I just decided, Ben says. It seemed silly not to. If I was curious.

– And now? Rick says.

– I don't know. I'd like to know if she's there.

– I thought you said she'd decided not to go back to him, Rick says.

– I don't know, Ben says. I thought so, yes.

They start to walk round the pond, the dog at their heels.

– I thought I'd just say hello, Ben says.

– Why not? Rick says.

– But now I don't know whether to phone again or not.

– Because you mean he might do the same thing again?

– Uhuh.

– Why not write?

– He might simply throw the letter away, Ben says. And then I wouldn't know if she'd got it and was deliberately not answering or had never got it and would have answered if she had.

– Well then phone, Rick says.

– The same thing could happen again.

The dog has disappeared. Ben whistles for him as they walk.

Rick looks at his watch.

The dog comes round a bend in the path ahead of them, his nose covered in dust.

– Good boy! Ben says, kneeling down and embracing him.

– Shall we go back? Rick says.

– I don't mind.

– Come on boy, Rick says.

They turn and begin to walk back. The dog doesn't move.

– Good boy! Rick says, stopping and looking back at him. – Good boy! Food's waiting!

The dog stands still, looking at them. – Come! Rick says. Come Em, come! Good boy! Good boy!

– Good boy Em, Ben says, patting his knees encouragingly. Come on boy! Come!

– He'll come as soon as he loses sight of us, Rick says, setting off again.

– I suppose, Ben says, hurrying after him, I could just phone and ask for her again and then if he puts me off again ask if she really is still living there.

– Why not? Rick says, quickening his pace.

– As if I knew nothing about their relationship and just thought she had a room there or something, Ben says, hurrying to keep up with him.

– Why not? Rick says again. He stops and looks back.

– But he could say yes and then not do anything about it if I left a message, Ben says, stepping a yard or two ahead of him.

– You could go out there and see her, Rick says. See for yourself.

– Oh I couldn't do that, Ben says.

– Why not?

– I wouldn't want to spy on her.

– Who said anything about spying?

– Well, Ben says, if I was snooping around waiting to catch a glimpse of her...

There is a sound of thundering feet and the dog is upon them. – Good boy! Rick says, hugging him. Good boy.

He disentangles the lead from his neck and snaps it on the dog's collar.

– I suppose I could try phoning once more, Ben says. And then decide.

– Why should he try to hide her from you? Rick asks as they head for home.

– I don't know, Ben says. I just had the feeling he was calling out in an empty house.

– On the phone?

– How do you mean, on the phone?

– You were able to sense that on the phone?

– You know how it is. There was a sort of echo.

– But if she was out it would be empty, wouldn't it?

– I just felt he was pretending to call, Ben says. He knew there was no one there and just pretended to call.

– Sit, Rick says.

The dog sits at once. They wait for a break in the traffic.

– One can get an impression of something like that, Ben says. Even at a distance.

– Come, Rick says. He takes his friend's arm and the three of them quickly cross the road.

– It's to do with echo, Ben says as they set off down the hill. Even on the phone you can sense the echo if a house is empty.

– Only if it's really empty, Rick says. If there isn't any furniture or anything.

– You can sense if someone is only pretending to call, Ben says.

– Oh yes, Rick says, you can always sense that.

– It's to do with a lack of belief in the call itself, Ben says. You can sense that on the phone.

– Oh yes, Rick says. You can sense that on the phone. Come on boy! he says, as the dog drags him sideways across the pavement.

– Especially if you're looking out for something funny, Ben says.

The dog pulls them down the hill.

* * *

– She went because her mother had sat there years before with some man she didn't even marry? Francesca says.

– Grandmother, Ben says.

– Grandmother then, Francesca says. It makes even less sense.

– It was important to her, Ben says.

– Do you understand what it was all about? Francesca asks Rick.

– In a way, he says. But –

– Went where? Robert asks.

– Don't interrupt, his mother says.

– Went where?

– To a garden in Siena, Ben says.

– What garden?

– Eat your supper, his father says.

– I have.

– You've still got some on your plate.

– It's bad.

– What do you mean bad?

– It's bad. Look at it.

– There's nothing wrong with it.

– The potatoes are black.

– Come on, his father says. Eat up.

– I can't. Look at it. It's all black.

– If there's a black spot in it, cut it out.

– I can't. It's all black.

– Robert, his father says.

– Dad!

– I'll give you another, his mother says.

– I don't want another. I'm not hungry any more.

– All right, his mother says. You can go out and play if you want.

– I want my pudding.

– Then finish what's on your plate first.

– It's bad. I want my pudding.

– All right, his mother says. You'll have it when I serve it up for all of us.

Robert pushes his plate away from him and rubs his mouth furiously with his napkin.

– It meant something to her, Ben says to Francesca. When she told me about it I could see it meant something. I just haven't been able to convey it properly.

She clears away their plates and brings the pudding to the table.

– It seems, Ben says, that the whole family was killed by the Nazis. The old mother, that is, and the brother and his wife and their children and him and his wife and children.

– How did she find out? Rick asks.

– I don't know. She may have been told. They were quite a well-known family in Trieste.

Robert holds out his empty plate.

123

– You want a second helping? his mother asks him.

He nods.

– Don't you have a tongue?

He nods again.

– Well?

– Please.

She refills his plate.

– She never saw him again? Rick asks.

– No, Ben says. He actually went on writing to her for a while but she never replied and eventually he stopped.

Robert holds out his empty plate again.

– No, his mother says. You've had enough.

– Please.

– No.

– Please, Mum!

– Go on, Rick says. Give him a spoonful.

– I think a cousin survived, Ben says. It may have been through him she heard.

– There, Francesca says. But no more. Understand?

– She was in touch with this cousin? Rick asks.

– I don't know, Ben says. She didn't say.

Robert licks his spoon and puts it down on his empty plate.

– Can I go now? he asks.

– Yes dear, his mother says. Fold your napkin.

– I think that's what made such an impression on her, Ben says.

– What? Rick says.

– That it might have been her grandfather and he was killed like that.

– He couldn't have been her grandfather, Francesca says. If they'd married she wouldn't have existed.

– One doesn't think like that, does one? Ben says.

– I said fold your napkin, Francesca says to her son.

– One can't imagine not being, Ben says. Only being slightly different.

– I said fold it, Francesca says. Come on. Don't be silly.

– I think that's what she was trying to understand, Ben says. Why the garden was so important to her.

– Because they died like that? Francesca says, folding her son's napkin and putting it in its ring.

– Because of everything, Ben says.

– I still don't get it, Francesca says.

– I haven't explained it very well.

– No, no. I probably didn't understand.

And, later, when he has gone, she says to Rick: – I really can't see what the fuss is about. He wasn't even her grandfather.

– That's just the point, isn't it? Rick says.

– Lots of people died in the war, she says. If one started to get upset because of every single one of them there'd be no end to it. I mean it would be different if she'd actually known this chap.

And when he is silent she says: – Explain it to me then. Explain to me just what you think the point is.

– I can't really, he says. But I think I understand what he means.

– Well if you understand then explain it to me.

– I can't, Fran, he says. If you don't see it you don't see it.

– I'm fed up with people being obsessed by the Holocaust, she says. It's done and we've got to move on.

– It's different if you're Jewish, Rick says.

– I don't see why, she says. I don't say we must forget. Only not make it an excuse for all sorts of private hang-ups.

– How do you mean an excuse?

– Just an excuse.

– How do you mean?

– Oh never mind, she says. If you don't see it you don't see it.

– Come on, Fran, he says. That's no way to argue.

– He's always like that, she says. He can't have a simple affair based on sex or mutual interests or anything. It always has to be these odd-ball things nobody understands and he gets tired of before the year's out.

– I don't know what you mean, he says.

– Don't you?

– No.

– Well with Sand it was because he was curious about how anyone could work for something called the Egg Marketing Board and with Henrietta it was because she'd been raped and he was sorry for her and with Nancy it was because her mother had been a tight-rope walker.

– Oh come on! he says.

– It's true, she says. Just think about it.

– And with you?

– That was just an adolescent crush, she says.

– Well, he says, we've all got our quirks.

– What's that supposed to mean?

– Nothing. Just what I said.

– Well, she says, all I can say is that some of us are a lot quirkier than others.

– I don't see why you say that.

– Don't you?

– No I don't, he says.

– Why do you always stand up for him like that? she says. You know basically you agree with me.

– I don't agree with you, he says. You always say that, as if I had to agree with you or be deliberately perverse.

– But you are, she says. You take the other side just to have an argument.

– You think I like arguing with you?

– I don't know why else you do it then.

– There you go again, he says.

– *I* go again?

– If what you say is true, he says, everybody would always be of the same opinion as everybody else. It's ridiculous.

– I didn't say everybody, she says. I said you and I.

– We always have to agree about everything?

– No. But we usually do. Only you won't admit it.

– That's ridiculous, Rick says.

And, later still, after he's walked the dog and they are putting out the lights downstairs, he says: – We've all got our quirks you know. You've got yours and I've got mine as much as he has his.

– All I can say then, she says, is that I'm glad I don't have his.

– So am I, he says. But there's no reason to be so dismissive of his.

– I wasn't dismissive, she says. I just said it didn't make sense to me.

– There's a lot of things about other people that don't make sense, he says. But that's no reason to dismiss them.

– What's the matter with you tonight? she says. I told you I wasn't dismissing him.

– I don't know what you were doing then, he says.

– I told you, she says. I just said I couldn't understand what all the fuss was about.

– It's not fuss, he says as he climbs into bed.

– All right, she says. I can't understand what this woman was on about or why he was so taken up by it.

– Perhaps she's beautiful, he says.

– I wouldn't get so upset for him if he fell for beautiful women, she says, putting out the light on her side of the bed. That would be understandable. But it's this other thing I find so peculiar.

– I don't see anything very seductive about working for the Egg Marketing Board, he says, putting out the light on his side and yawning.

– That's exactly it, she says. Don't you see? It intrigued him that anyone could work for something so unseductive.

– She was quite striking though, he says after a while.

– Who?

– Sand.

– Sand? You found her striking?

– She's a striking woman. Of course she is.

– Only a man could see her as striking, she says.

– I'm speaking as a man, he says, yawning again.

– I thought she was vulgar beyond belief, she says.

– Did you?

– Yes.

– Ah, he says, but this time the word is engulfed by a third, enormous yawn.

X   Edmund Spencer

– I didn't think you'd come, he says.

   – Why?

   – I don't know. I just didn't.

She is silent, looking down at her feet.

   – First, he says, I didn't think you'd call back. Then I didn't think you'd come.

   – Why didn't you think I'd call back?

   – I don't know. I wasn't even sure if you were still there. If you remember, the last time we spoke you said you might not go back.

   – I couldn't leave Bess, she says. I really couldn't.

   – So you're prepared to put up with Frank for the sake of the dog?

   – Oh, she says, it's not like that.

They start to walk along the Embankment towards Westminster Bridge.

   – Why didn't you think I'd call you back?

   – I don't know.

   – I was out at my Yoga. Then it was too late to call you that evening.

– Anyway, he says, here you are.

– Here I am, she says.

– Everything's back to where it was before.

She laughs.

– Did you ever finish *The Ambassadors*? she asks.

– No. I'll have to start again next year.

– You could always read it when you're not on holiday.

– No, he says. It's my holiday book. I'll finish it one day.

They walk.

– You told your mother? he asks.

– Told her what?

– About seeing the garden.

– No.

– But I thought – ?

– I never talked about it with her, she says. I don't even know if Granny ever told her.

– I see, he says. But you never asked her if she knew? If they *had* talked about it?

– No, she says. She's a different kind of person altogether.

– Yes but still...

– She's mainly interested in her health.

They walk.

– And you? he says. Have you understood what you were looking for there?

She laughs.

– Have you?

– Not really, she says.

– I've been thinking about it, he says.

– You?

– It's as if you'd given me something to think about. Literally.

130

She laughs.

They climb the steps to the bridge, cross the road and go down the steps to the other side.

– To be honest, she says, a horrible suspicion has begun to dawn on me.

– Oh? he says.

– About the garden.

– What about it?

– I think it may not have been the right one.

– Not the right one?

– But it doesn't matter, she says. Does it?

– I don't know, he says. I...

– It was at the airport, she says. I was thinking about it all and I suddenly heard Granny's voice saying on the south side of town and this one was west.

– How do you know?

They draw aside to let a group of joggers pass.

– When the sun set it was between the sun and the town, she says, when they resume their walk.

– That's all very vague, he says.

– I looked at the map, she says. I found monuments in the guide book they said they were in the south part of town. It wasn't where the hotel was.

– You're sure she said south?

– I think so. Yes.

– You don't think she made a mistake.

– She could have. But why be so precise?

– But there couldn't be two hotels in Siena with that sort of garden, he says.

– If there was one, she says, why not two?

He is silent, at her side.

– That must have been the pattern, mustn't it? she says.

In the old palazzos. Build them on the edge of the plateau with a garden stretching out at the back, looking out over the valley to the hills beyond.

Another group of joggers forces them up against the embankment wall.

– It doesn't matter though, does it? she says, when they are walking again. Even if it wasn't Siena but San Gimignano, say.

– But, he says, if you sat there and began to feel that you understood something about your life and why you …and then you…

– I don't think it matters, she says. But I felt I had to tell you.

– Why?

– Because you'd listened. Because you'd helped me to talk about it. I didn't want to think…

– I wouldn't ever have known, would I? he says.

– I just felt bad, she says. I felt like a fraud.

– So that's why you said you were glad I'd rung?

– Yes.

They walk on towards Lambeth Bridge.

– Is Sandra all right now? she asks.

– Sandra? I wouldn't know.

– Oh?

– I don't see her any more, he says.

– You mean…?

– Yes.

She is silent.

They reach Lambeth Bridge and stop.

– So it *was* a mistake, she says. Going to the mountains.

– Why a mistake?

– Well if –. Oh, she says. I see.

132

– I feel a lot better myself, he says.

They lean against the embankment wall and look down at the river.

– What about your father? he asks.

– What about him?

– He's well?

– He's always well, she says. He likes to let you know it too.

They watch the driftwood glide past.

– They went walking in the Himalayas, she says.

– Who did?

– My father and his family.

– Really?

– Remarkable, he said it was.

– What was remarkable about it?

– Oh, she says, everything.

He is silent.

– You've seen him then? he says at last.

– Him?

– Your father.

– I go there for lunch on the first Sunday of every month, she says.

– I didn't realize it was that regular.

– My father likes regularity.

– And you?

– Me?

– I mean, how did it feel, seeing him after your experience in the garden and everything?

– It was interesting, she said. I tried to measure the distance between us. To see if it had made any difference.

– And had it?

– Yes, she says.

– In what way?

– I don't know, she says. I just feel more established in my difference now I've been there. Do you understand?

– Yes, he says. I think so. But if it wasn't even…?

– I told you, she says. That doesn't matter. It was sitting there and feeling the place and feeling how it must have been all those years ago and feeling time sort of standing still before starting to flow again.

– And then you came back to the same life, he says.

– That's what made it possible, she says.

– How possible?

– I don't know how to explain, she says.

They watch the boats move slowly past them.

– I suppose it's to do with a past, she says. Having your own past and nobody else's. This is you. There isn't anyone else like that. There never was and never will be. So it's a responsibility.

He is silent.

– You remember when we talked about Absalom? she says. That first evening?

– Of course, he says.

– He had his hair, she says. No one else had hair like that.

– I had a look at that passage, he says. With a father like that what else could he do?

– He chose to act as he did, she says. He chose to do that with his hair.

– But that past, he says. What you told me about it. It has nothing to do with you, does it? It was just an episode in your grandmother's life. It may not even have happened as she told it.

– It doesn't matter, she says. That day was a turning point for her. And for me.

– But it didn't change anything.

– It did for me, she says.

He is silent.

– Shall we go back? she says.

They turn back in the direction of the Festival Hall.

– Not just that day as she told it, she says. But everything that happened afterwards.

– You mean his death?

– Everything, she says.

– You see, she says, it's the silence that's so frightening. This man who sent a donkey and then more and more letters, which she never answered. And then his life was snuffed out. And all that's left is what my grandmother told me about that garden.

– But what kind of a man was he? he says. First he's engaged and then he's rushing after your grandmother and promising to meet her when she comes back to Italy and then he's back with his fiancée but still writing to her. Does his death really make all that meaningful?

– What's meaningful? she says.

They climb the steps and recross Westminster Bridge.

– Anyway, she says, when something like that happens it makes you think not just about your own past but about that of Jews as a whole.

– Why not mankind? he says. Why stop at Jews?

– One can't think in those terms, she says. At least I can't. It's too vague. It doesn't mean anything.

– And the past of Jews means something?

– To me, yes, she says.

– But you told me you don't believe.

– Not in God, no.

– Well then.

– God has nothing to do with it.

– How can you talk about Jews without talking about God?

– It's easy, she says.

– You mean they were deluded?

– It doesn't matter to me whether they were or they weren't, she says. What happened to the Jews in the past and then in this century – that's alive for me. Through him.

– It came to me at the airport, she says. Why it was so important, that garden. It's as if that day their whole lives were present to them, their lives before and their lives after. Everything that would happen and not happen and all that would happen and not happen to their descendants. Everything. Enclosed in that garden. Held together by the trees and the wall and the silence. That's why I had to go there. To feel it for myself.

– Except that it was the wrong garden.

– It doesn't matter where it was, she says. The important thing is that everything came together in a single moment in a single enclosed spot. And if I could really feel it, really understand it, then perhaps I could understand why I was alive and what I had to do.

– And do you?

– Of course not, she says.

They walk in silence.

– One never does, she says, does one?

He points with his foot: – Look. They take the trouble to cut quotations into the concrete and then they can't even spell the names of the poets right. Sweet Thames run softly till I end my song. Edmund Spencer. With a cee. That's the nineteenth-century philosopher. And he was called Herbert, not Edmund.

– I'd never noticed, she says.

– It's new, he says. Part of the general refurbishment. But they're like bad imitators pretending to be part of a tradition. Everything's a little bit wrong.

– Of course, he says, the Elizabethans weren't too worried about spelling and Spenser may even sometimes have spelt his name with a cee, but somehow I don't think whoever did this was sophisticated enough to be trying to draw that to our attention.

They walk on.

– Isn't it strange, he says, that we should be walking here like this and talking about life and death and God as if we were talking about the weather.

– How else should one talk about it?

– I don't know, he says. It's just strange.

They draw level with the Festival Hall.

– So, he says, you've gone back after all.

– Back?

– To Frank. Your life.

– For the moment, she says. Yes.

– Just for the moment?

– The crisis comes, she says, and then it passes. And one just goes on. Nothing ever really clears up though one keeps thinking it will. And then the sense of crisis recedes. For a little while at least.

– I thought you said you'd found a new strength, he says. In your difference.

– From my father, she says. Yes.

They stop and look at the river.

– Anyway, she says, one says things like that. One even

137

believes it. But it's the jargon of the time, isn't it?

– It doesn't correspond to anything?

– I don't know, she says. At moments I suppose one thinks it does. But one can never really step outside, can one, and really see things clearly?

She glances at her watch.

– I have to go, she says.

– Now? he says. I thought we might have a cup of coffee.

– No. I'm sorry. I have to go.

– Home?

– I've got some shopping to do.

– I see.

She stands beside him.

– Which way are you going? he asks her.

– I'll walk over Hungerford Bridge.

– I'll come with you.

– No. Please.

She holds out her hand: – Thank you. For agreeing to see me.

– Well it was you who…

– Goodbye.

He takes her hand: – Goodbye.

She turns and hurries up the stairs. He stands, watching her, waiting for her to turn at the top and wave to him.

XI   Like That Mountain

Later, in the kitchen in Putney, he says to Francesca:
– I didn't know how to take it.
  – How do you mean, take it?
  – It was so abrupt, he says. She just held out her hand
and walked away. She didn't even look back when she
got to the top of the steps.
  – And so?
  – I don't know if she hoped I'd ask to see her again or
if she was just relieved to have got it over with.
  – Over with?
  – Meeting me and all that.
  – She needn't have if she hadn't wanted to.
  – That's what I've been thinking. But then she left so
abruptly.
  – Do you want to see her again? she asks him.
  – I don't know.
  – Well if you don't who does?
  – I didn't think I did, he says. When we were walking
along. I thought I should never have phoned her. I didn't

know what I was doing walking along there beside her and listening to all that stuff about gardens and being Jewish and all the rest of it. But when she said goodbye like that I couldn't believe it.

– Couldn't believe what?

– That it was finished. As if she hadn't talked to me about anything that mattered at all. As if we'd met for some sort of business deal and when it was concluded that was it, there was nothing to say except goodbye.

– You told me yourself, Francesca says, it's like that when one meets people on holiday. Or on a boat.

– You know that garden she talked about?

– Yes?

– She told me she thought she might have made a mistake.

– A mistake?

– That perhaps it wasn't the one.

– Wasn't the one what?

– Wasn't the one her grandmother had talked about. Had sat in with that man.

– But I thought that was the whole point, she says.

– Yes, he says. So did I.

– When she first saw the place, he says, she knew that was why she'd come to Italy. And then she sat in it and tried to imagine what it had been like all those years before and what it meant that this man who'd been killed by the Nazis later wasn't her grandfather and all the rest of it. And then later she began to have doubts. At the airport, she said. This garden was on the west side of the town and she suddenly remembered her grandmother saying south. That's why she wanted to see me. To tell me she might have been wrong.

– Couldn't her grandmother have been wrong about south?

– She didn't seem to feel it mattered anyway, he says. Whether it was the real one or not. But she wanted to tell me.

– Why?

– That's all she wanted to see me for, he says. To tell me it might not have been the one.

– Yes but why?

– Just to salve her conscience, he says.

– I'm afraid you've lost me, she says.

– Fran, he says, do you think I should try to see her again?

– If you want to.

– I don't know, he says.

– No one else does, she says.

– Is it just me, he says, or is it our whole society? That makes things so difficult I mean. That makes us have to decide things all the time. Even something as simple as seeing someone again.

– I don't know what you mean, she says.

– Well, he says, scratching at the spot on the table, if you just bumped into people in the course of things and so on it would be simple. But it never seems to be like that with me. I have to decide and choose and phone and write and then it makes it all so much more meaningful than it should be.

– Why?

– Because then if I don't feel particularly pleased to see them I feel guilty at having phoned or written and so on. Can't you see that?

– Why make so many problems for yourself? she says.

141

– And I can't get over this business of speech, he says. One talks about things that could change one's life but it's just like talking about the weather. Everything one says seems to remain equally trivial. Do you know what I mean?

– If you ask me, she says, you don't really want to be bothered with her. But for some reason you've persuaded yourself that you should.

– Why can't it be just like that mountain? he says.

– Like what mountain?

– The one we walked round. Just solid and big and out there. But life doesn't seem to be like that. You think you're advancing and then you find you've been standing still. You imagine you've been standing still and you find you've gone backwards. Except you no longer know what's back and what's front and why you're doing what you're doing in the first place.

– Anyway, she says, didn't you say she was still with her chap?

– Yes, he says. But I don't think she'll be there for long.

– Why not wait then and let her get in touch with you?

– And if she doesn't?

– Then that's it, she says. She doesn't want to.

– But if she does but she's shy?

– That's a risk you'll have to take, she says.

– I thought of that, he says. I thought though I'd probably get more obsessed if I waited for her to get in touch and she didn't. I wouldn't be able to forgive myself.

– Forgive yourself for what?

– After all, he says, it's such a little thing, isn't it, writing her a note?

– Then go ahead, she says. If you feel like that.

– I thought that's what you'd say.

– What else can I say?

– I don't know, Fran, he says. I really don't know. If only one could see ahead, he says. From the point of view of my grandchildren, for example. It would all seem so inevitable. They wouldn't even question it.

– So you've already got grandchildren? she says. And you've only seen her twice in your life?

– A bit more than that, he says. Anyway, I didn't say they'd be her grandchildren.

– Nobody looks ahead like that, she says. People only do things because they seem right at the time. Sometimes they are and sometimes they aren't. You only discover that later.

– It wasn't always like that, he says. In the history of the world I mean.

– Wasn't it? she says.

– You think it was? You don't think this is a twentieth-century thing?

– I wouldn't know, she says.

– I suppose it can't be, can it, he says, if you've never had that feeling yourself.

– I may just have been lucky, she says. Or unimaginative.

He goes on scratching with his nail at the mark on the table.

– Perhaps I'll phone her then, he says after a while. She can always say no. I just don't want it to end like that, he says. With a handshake in the street.

– Then how do you want it to end? she says. With tears in a café?

– Are those the alternatives? he asks her.

– With grandchildren then? she says.

– I suppose so, he says. Yes. I'm fed up with all this phoning and writing and deciding.

– That's another issue, she says.

– Is it?

– You just want someone to take away the need to make decisions, she says. What sort of a basis is that for anything?

– I didn't say that, he says. You generalize and then of course it's ridiculous.

– Did you feel that way about Sand?

– No, he says. Yes. At first perhaps. I don't know.

– You don't?

– I don't know how we got into all this, he says. I only meant to ask you if you thought I should phone her again or not. I thought with your feminine intuition you'd be able to help me.

– I wasn't there, she says. I don't know the woman. Perhaps you should ask yourself.

– She just put out her hand, he says. Then she walked away. She didn't even turn at the top of the stairs.

– You think she meant it when she said she'd only wanted to see you again to tell you it might not have been the right garden?

– I don't know, Fran, he says. At times I thought I could understand even the things she wasn't saying. At others I didn't even know how to take the things she was saying.

– It's not the end of the world, she says. Don't look so sad. Just see her again.

– You think I should?

– You know you're going to try.

– Am I? he says. You think I am?

– Come on, she says. Don't play games with yourself.

– Perhaps I shouldn't, he says. I don't know her really. I don't know what she wants out of life. I don't know what she wants out of other people. I don't know if she even noticed me really. I was just someone to talk to. Anyone would have done.

– Try seeing her again, she says. Then you'll find out.

– I think it's because she's so concerned about something, he says. That's what I responded to. That she was struggling with something. That's what I responded to. That's what I want to get hold of. Do you understand? He gloried in his hair and so he was hanged by his hair. Is that true or isn't it?

– What are you talking about? she says.

– Something she said. About Absalom.

– Absalom who?

– In the Bible. Then she asked me if I thought it really could be like that. And I'd never really thought about it.

– You're talking to yourself, she says. And when he doesn't reply she says: – Go ahead. You can phone from here.

– I'll give it a couple of days, he says. Just to make sure.

– Do that, she says. But don't ask me again.

– Yes, he says. That's what I'll do. I'll give it a couple of days and see what I feel like then.

XII   An End in Itself

Later, when she has put Robert to bed and Rick has taken
the dog for his last walk and they are sitting in the kitchen
having a cup of tea, she says to him: – He went on at me
about whether he should see her again or not.

– And what did you advise him?

– How could I advise him? she says. Whatever he does
it'll be wrong.

– Why wrong?

– It always is. He thinks about it too much. It's all
theoretical with him.

– He seemed quite keen on her, he says.

– He was quite keen on me once, she says. Remember?

– Human beings have been known to fall in love more
than once, he says.

– Oh for God's sake, she says. He doesn't know her.
He's only obsessed with this garden of hers. And it turns
out not even to be the right one.

– It might be the right one, he says.

– Oh, it might be! she says.

– I don't think it matters anyway, he says, whether it's the right one or not.

– That's what he said, she says. That's what this woman feels. She makes some mystical thing out of it as far as I can see and he gets taken in by it. I'd have thought it mattered quite a lot myself whether it was the right one or not.

– I don't think you're being fair, he says. It doesn't seem to be a mystical thing at all with her.

– Oh? she says. What is it then?

– It's not mystical.

– All right then, she says. Take her side.

– I'm not taking anyone's side, he says. I just don't feel it's all that mystical.

– Tell me what it is then.

– I don't know, he says.

He pushes his cup across to her and she refills it.

– Perhaps, he says, if he starts to see more of her we'll find out what it is.

– I don't think he will.

– Why do you say that?

– I just don't think he will.

– Well we'll see, he says.

– Anyway, she says, there'll always be another woman with another garden.

– I don't know what you mean, he says.

– Yes you do, she says.

He swallows down his tea and pushes the cup across the table to her.

– More?

– No thanks. I'm exhausted. I think I'll just fall into bed.

147

– Me too, she says. If only he knew how these intense conversations of his wear out his friends.

– He's all right, he says.

– Of course he is. I just wish we could help him.

– He likes it, he says. He likes talking to you. It's an end in itself.

– And to you, she says.

– And to me.

But later, in the darkness of their bedroom, with just the thin stripe of light from the street lamp cutting across the ceiling, she says: – Do you know anything about Absalom's hair?

– Mmmmnnnn? he says.

She turns over on her back and stares up into the dark. After all their years together she knows when he is asleep and when he isn't. – In the Bible, she says. He gloried in his hair and so he was hanged by his hair.

He is breathing deeply and steadily at her side, in the way he does when he is trying to get to sleep.

– Do you? she says.

And then she realizes that for once she is wrong and he is actually already asleep.

GABRIEL JOSIPOVICI was born in Nice in 1940, lived in Egypt from 1945 to 1956, then came to England. He read English at Oxford. His plays have been widely performed and broadcast, and his recent book about reading the Bible, *The Book of God*, was widely acclaimed. He is Professor of English at the School of European Studies at Sussex University.